"5-Stars! Ms. L'Amour wraps up this riveting story with lots of drama, action, and intense passion that'll have you on the edge of your seat until the very last page!"

—Maria Loves Books Book Blog.

"The sexual tension between Gloria and Jaime is incredible, sensual, and steamy, and kept me wanting more, more, more!"

—The Book Enthusiast

"This romance is spectacular. It is witty and smart, will leave you breathless and wanting more."

—Mary Elizabeth's Crazy Book Obsession

"I don't think there could have been a better ending to this book. It was serious awesomeness, plenty of drama, heartbreak, jawdropping OMG, swooning, and happy smiles."

—Book Boyfriend Reviews

"Nelle certainly shows imagination when it comes to writing sex scenes and she even surpasses Gloria's Secret with this sequel."

—Arianne Richmonde, Bestselling Author of The Pearl Series.

"Bravo to you, Nelle L'Amour...I was addicted and fighting every impulse to flip to the last page to relieve the intense pressure and intense pressure to know how this story was going to end."

—The Book Blog

BOOKS BY NELLE L'AMOUR

Seduced by the Park Avenue Billionaire

Undying Love

Gloria's Secret

Gloria's Revenge

Dewitched (writing as E.L. Sarnoff)

Unhitched (writing as E.L. Sarnoff)

GLORIA'S REVENGE

GLORIA'S REVENGE

Nelle L'Amour

NICHOLS CANYON PRESS
Los Angeles, CA USA

Gloria's Secret
By Nelle L'Amour

ISBN-13: 978-1494353711
ISBN-10: 1494353717

Cover and Interior: Streetlight Graphics

To my readers. Without you, I couldn't be a writer.

"Three things cannot be hidden for long—
the sun, the moon, and the truth."

—Isabella S.,
my fourteen-year-old daughter

GLORIA'S REVENGE

Chapter 1

I COULDN'T BELIEVE I WAS IN Paris sitting in a cabin on the top of the famous Grande Roue Ferris wheel with Jaime Zander, staring wide-eyed at a magnificent two-stoned diamond ring that he'd just presented to me. I was in shock. We'd known each other for less than a week. My heart was fluttering as fast as a hummingbird's wings. Seated pantiless on his lap with my long legs draped over his muscular thighs, I was waiting for him to answer my question: "Are you asking me to marry you?"

Jaime's reaction was as intense as my own. He visibly jerked and blinked his denim blue eyes several times. And then he just gazed at me, hard and deep. A long second passed. With my heart still pounding, I waited with baited breath for his response. The silence of the night air was numbing.

"Gloria...no," he finally stuttered.

His words hit me with a blow. My face turned fifty shades of red. I felt foolishly embarrassed. It was time to mentally hit the "reset" button.

Except I didn't know what to say. And it appeared that he didn't either. Our brains were not communicating with our mouths. After a few moments, he regained his composure and broke the awkward stretch of silence. "It's a *toi et moi* ring."

A "you and me" ring, I said to myself. The lyrics of the Charles Aznavour song that had been playing when we'd arrived at the Ferris wheel floated in my head...*you and me, two hearts merge.* Except he wasn't giving me his heart. My emotions were a jumble of pain, self-loathing, and confusion.

He lifted the ring from the box. "I found it in an antiques shop on my way to my client. The dealer told me it's almost a hundred years old. An old soul like you. Do you like it?"

I gazed at the intricate, sparkling ring. "It's beautiful," I stammered. It truly was. An Art-Nouveau work of art, the two perfect heart-shaped diamonds kissing each other like lovers.

He grasped my right hand "Gloria, why are you shaking so much?"

"I'm just a little chilled," I lied, flinging my pashmina shawl across my right shoulder with my free hand. Inside, I was falling apart like a glacier-struck cruise ship. Confession: At this very moment, I hated this man—this man who I thought I loved—for how fucked up he could make me feel.

Without a blink, I watched as he slipped the ring onto my middle finger. It fit perfectly. I should have been thrilled that this man that I'd known for not even a week was giving me such an extravagant gift, but instead I found myself battling tears. *Don't cry, Gloria,* the inner me pleaded. *Please don't cry.*

"Thank you," I managed. Truthfully, I wanted to tear if off my finger and toss it into the Seine.

He planted a warm kiss on my lips. The kiss sent another chill through me, not the good kind.

I pulled away. My thumb nervously rubbed across

the smooth surface of the two entwining diamonds. "What is this ring for?"

Jaime coiled a lock of my long, loose hair around his hand and cocked a smile. "Working together. We're going to make a great team, Gloria."

So that's what I was—a client with benefits. A good fuck who made him money. A knife sliced through my heart. I may have foolishly thought I was in love with him, but he was clearly not in love with me.

The big wheel started spinning again, and as it spun back to earth, my emotions spun out of control. I buried my head into his chest, and unbeknownst to him, a tear sunk into his soft leather jacket.

Over the past six days, he had fucked my brains out. I had enjoyed every minute. Now, he was fucking *with* my brain. And I didn't like it one bit. There was a fine line between losing control and being out of control, and I had just crossed it.

Chapter 2

MORNING COULDN'T HAVE COME FAST enough. Showered and dressed, I was ready to go back to Los Angeles. I needed to get back to work and away from this man who had battered me both emotionally and physically. Taking a break from packing, I glanced at him, still asleep in bed. He looked so peaceful—a sharp contrast to the tense, conflicted me. And oh so beautiful. Sleeping on his back, with the covers draped low on his hips, he offered me a bird's-eye view of his toned pecs and arms, washboard abs, and that magnificent V that led to the tent beneath the sheets that told me he'd had a hard-on in his sleep. And oh, that gorgeous chiseled face with its kissable dimpled chin. My chest tightened. I had to look away.

Folding up the lingerie that he'd rummaged through and made a mess of yesterday, I silently cursed the soreness between my inner thighs. Not because I found the pain uncomfortable but because I found the memory associated with it unbearable. He had fucked me silly on the Grande Roue, sending me orbiting, and then had put my emotions into a tailspin.

Jaime Fucking Zander had gotten under my skin and then into my bloodstream. And somehow, he'd gotten into my heart. Both my beloved late mentor, Madame Paulette, and good friend, Sandrine, were right. I'd fallen in love with him. Except this complicated, commitment-phobic womanizer, whose name meant "I love" in French, was incapable of loving. I was just one of his many conquests. I glanced down at the ring on my middle finger. Caught in the ray of sunshine that beamed through the French windows of our charming hotel room, its sparkle was blinding. Once again, my thumb involuntarily skimmed over the two magnificent kissing diamond hearts. *Toi et moi.* He probably gave this kind of ring to all his hook-ups. I just wanted to go back to being *moi.* Gloria Long, the cool, confident CEO of Gloria's Secret, the world's largest retailer of lingerie. The powerhouse of a woman in control of her life. Yes, heading up a billion dollar, global empire came with its share of challenges and headaches, but it didn't come with lust and heartbreak. My eyes shot back to Jaime. Damn him! He had made my emotions spin totally out of control. I couldn't focus on anything but him. Even light packing was an effort.

My unrest was compounded by my fatigue. I was eager for my coffee to arrive. While he had slept like a baby, I'd tossed and turned all night. I didn't sleep a wink. There was only one good thing about insomnia—you can't have nightmares—and at least, Boris Borofsky stayed out of my brainwaves. I kept replaying the events of the week in my head. My first encounter with Jaime in the elevator of The Walden in New York. Our swim in the hotel pool and our mind-blowing shower in the men's locker room. Dinner in his room where he feasted on me. His pitch for my account followed by blindfolding me and fucking me on his conference room table. And then after I caught him heatedly kissing my assistant, Vivien Holden, he followed me to Paris to tell me the truth. That Vivien was his manipulative stepsister and her father, Victor, Gloria's Secret Chairman of the Board, his abusive stepfather. He had rescued me from Victor's drunken, sexual assault and from that moment on, we were inseparable. Two lovers who couldn't get enough of each other.

Jaime Zander had consumed me. The truth: I couldn't get enough of him. But as I folded the blue chiffon dress that I'd worn last night, I knew in the end I was only going to get hurt. Once a player, always a player. Having won our account with his brilliant BDSM-inspired pitch—*Gloria's Secret. Let yourself be carried away*—I now dreaded having to work with him. How should I proceed? There was only one answer: I had to go back—and keep it pure business. One of Madame Paulette's favorite songs had been Edith Piaf's "Je ne Regrette Rien." The intoxicating scent of him was still on my dress and assaulted my senses. Tears stung my eyes. I suddenly regretted everything. Everything that had to do with Jaime Zander.

"Hey, Angel, what are you doing?" a raspy voice from behind me called out. My skin bristled. He was up.

Without turning around to look at him, I said, "Packing. The vacation's over. I'm going back to LA, and you're going back to New York."

I heard him climb out of bed. "Where'd you go last night?" he asked with a sleepy yawn. "I reached for you, but you weren't there."

"I went to sleep in the other bed. I had insomnia."

"Did I keep you up?" His voice was getting closer.

"Yes." That was a fact. I didn't elaborate.

As I zipped up my Vuitton overnight case, two strong bare arms slipped under my armpits and wrapped around my breasts. He cupped the full mounds in his palms and massaged them. My tender nipples hardened and elongated beneath his touch. How quickly he could make my core ache. Damn him! I whirled around and faced him. The effect his bedroom eyes, gorgeous stubbled face, and tousled bedhead hair had on me was unraveling me. *Collect yourself, Gloria. Don't let him do this to you.*

"We need to have a serious conversation," I spluttered, thankful that he was wearing pajama bottoms.

"Seriously?"

His deliberate or not play on words got under my skin.

"Yes." I hissed the word.

He ran his long fingers through my still loose platinum hair. He was doing everything that got me all riled up. "About what?"

I jerked away. "About *toi et moi.*"

He let out that deep, sexy chortle that always undid me. "Your French accent is perfect, Gloria. Just like you."

I tried hard not to react. *Just tell him what's on your mind. Not what's in your heart.*

I sucked in a gulp of air. "I think we need to keep our relationship strictly business. There's too much riding on the line."

He cocked a brow. "What do you mean by that?"

What I mean is that you're taking me down a collision course. There's only disaster at the finish line. I can't afford to be a wreck.

What I said: "I'm under a lot of pressure to take Gloria's Secret to the next level. With all the competition springing up, Wall Street is scrutinizing us. There are a lot of people out there who want to see me fail...including Victor."

His jaw tensed at the mention of his stepfather's name. "So..."

I jumped right in. "I think you should stop fucking me, and we'll pretend that none of this happened."

Jaime knitted his eyebrows as if in deep thought. He spoke sooner than I thought he would. "You're the client, Gloria. And the client's needs come first. Except I think your needs are different than what you think."

"What do you mean by that?" I asked, echoing his earlier line.

"I. Think. You. Need. Me."

A tug at my hair accompanied each punctuated word. The way he looked straight into my eyes made my heart patter. I was losing my cool. Several long seconds passed before I responded.

"No, Mr. Zander, what I need is a successful advertising campaign." *And my sanity back.* "And by the way, I don't want to be in it in any shape or form."

Jaime shrugged his shoulders. "A big mistake, in my humble opinion, Ms. Long. You should learn to trust me. I thought you were doing a great job, but obviously you've regressed for some reason."

Inside me, unexpected sadness mixed with my hormones. It took all I had to keep it together.

"And I think you should take your ring back." I started to twist it off my finger, but I think because my period was coming, my fingers were swollen from water retention. I couldn't get it past my knuckle. "Damn it," I cursed silently.

He tipped my head up by my chin. My pained eyes met darkened pools of blue. I frantically continued to pull at the ring.

"Listen, Gloria, I don't want the ring back. It's not returnable." With his other hand, he squeezed my right hand, trapping my fidgeting fingers and the ring in his fist.

"You can sell it on eBay or pawn it." I grinded the words between clenched teeth.

His thickly lashed eyelids lowered. He looked wounded. "No, Gloria, I have no time or interest in doing that. And it'll never fetch the price I paid."

I suddenly felt bad. He had, beyond doubt, paid an exorbitant amount of money for it. It was a rare antique...unique and special. Two magnificent entwined diamond hearts. Priceless.

"Gloria, I want you to have it." I stood frozen as he softened his grip around my hand and raised it to his lips. He placed a warm, reverent kiss on the ring, grazing my flesh, and then gazed into my eyes.

"Just accept it as a souvenir from Paris. And the kiss too."

My heart was beating so loudly I was sure he could hear it. To my relief, there was a loud knock at the door saving me from responding. "That must be the coffee. I'll go get it."

Freeing myself, I scurried to the door and opened it. Yes, my coffee. With a cheerful *"bonjour,"* the waiter entered our chamber and set a silver tray with the coffee onto a small round table. After taking care of him, I busied myself pouring two cups of the steamy dark liquid—one for Jaime, the other for me. The smell of the rich caffeine wafted into my nose. I generously poured steamed milk into both cups of the aromatic brew, remembering that he liked his coffee café au lait style like me. As the warm, frothy liquid filled his cup, I reflected on how much I already knew about this man in just a week's time.

He strode toward me. "Great. Coffee for *toi et moi*."

Toi et moi. The words echoed in my head. There was no *toi et moi*. Yet, my core was aching, throbbing. Unwanted tears were verging. I needed to get away from him. "I'll be right back. I need to use the bathroom."

"I'll be waiting for you." He smiled warmly and took a sip of the steaming coffee.

Inside the bathroom, I sat on the toilet longer than I needed. I finally grabbed a thick wad of toilet paper. I wiped my still throbbing folds and took a look, hoping not to see the first sign of my period. The last thing I needed was to fly home with soaked tampons and cramps. I breathed a soft sigh of relief when I saw no trace of blood. But my heart grew heavy. Jaime's creamy cum was in my face. The memories of fucking him last night on the Grande Roue flooded my head. Oh my God! That explosive, mind-blowing orgasm. As I relived it, my core morphed into the Eiffel Tower cackling with white lights. How could I live without this man inside me? I was second-guessing my decision to end our intimacy—would it end up being the worst business decision of my life? A tear of despair trickled down my face.

The sound of a phone ringing brought me back to the moment. It was either Jaime's mobile or mine; we had identical iPhones. When it stopped on the second ring, I knew it was his. I heard him say hello, and then the flush of the toilet and the subsequent running of water to wash my hands blocked out the sound of his voice.

When I stepped back into the bedroom, Jaime was still on the phone. He was pacing and the expression on his face was intense. Avoiding eye contact, he lowered his voice and said, "I've got to go. I'll see you in LA, babe."

As he ended the call, my heart skipped a beat. "Who were you talking to?"

"Another client." His voice wavered.

Rage and jealousy crescendoed inside me. "Oh, so do you call all your female clients 'angel' or 'babe'?"

He winked. "Just the ones I find attractive."

I cringed. I wanted to grab his cell phone and smack him with it. My second-guess thoughts evaporated like water. I had made the right decision. He was a rogue. A player. Except he wasn't going to play with me. No fucking way.

"Mr. Zander, from now on in please only call me Ms. Long."

"Is that what I should shout out when you make me come?"

I screwed up my face. *Smartass!*

He smirked at me.

Let him smirk. I braided my hair. I was back to being in control.

∽

Wouldn't you know, our private planes were scheduled to depart at almost the same time. When my driver didn't show up on time, Jaime offered me a ride in his limo.

"I'll take a taxi," I huffed as I stood in front of the hotel with him.

"Bonne chance, Ms. Long," he said nonchalantly. "Have you ever tried to catch a cab in Paris morning rush hour traffic?"

I was about to find out. Wearing black leggings, a sweater, and ballet flats, I darted to the edge of the insanely busy Saint-Germain, and started to hail a cab. I jumped up and down, flailing my arms, trying to get one to stop. "Taxi!" I repeatedly shouted on the top of my lungs. I must have looked like some kind of whacked-out ballerina dancing to a symphony of honking horns. One cab after another whooshed by without stopping. I continued with my desperate dance, growing more and more frustrated by the minute. When cab number-I-don't-know-what zoomed by me, I turned my head and stole a glance at Jaime. He was smirking. The asshole! He was enjoying every minute of my pathetic song-and-dance show. I wrinkled my nose at him. To my utter chagrin, he mock-mimicked me.

Fuck him. It was time to get aggressive. Convinced the cab drivers weren't seeing me, I stepped deeper into the crazy-with-traffic Paris boulevard.

"Atten-cion!" screamed a voice. I processed the word in my brain—"Watch Out!"— but it was too late. I cranked my head to the left. A stubby Frenchman on a motorbike was speeding my way. In fact, he

was only a few feet away. I froze.

As the cursing biker zoomed toward me, I said good-bye to this world. My life was flashing by me. Suddenly, I felt someone yank me out of harm's way and scoop me up into strong arms. It all happened so fast. Dazed, I gazed up at my savior. Familiar blue eyes met mine. Jaime Zander had saved my life.

"You're coming with me," he ordered as his black Peugeot pulled up to the front of the hotel.

I sunk my head into his taut chest. Update: I was back to being out of control.

I sat as far away as possible from him in the back seat of the chauffeured sedan as we cruised down the A2 en route to Le Bourget Airport. I busied myself with my iPhone, catching up on texts and e-mails. He sat smugly reading the *International Herald Tribune.* Despite the silence between us, I could still hear little electrical sparks buzzing in the air. The effect this sex god had on me was infuriating and couldn't be denied.

"Aren't you even going to thank me for saving your life?" he asked without as much as lifting his head up from the newspaper.

"Thanks." I scrunched up my face and hissed the word at him.

"You're welcome, *Ms. Long.*"

The snarky way he said my name made my skin bristle. Mr. Polite just knew how to get to me. Working with him was going to be a nightmare. I just knew it.

I gazed down at the double diamond ring on my

finger. Even more breathtaking in the daytime, the two entwined hearts glistened. The ring was an antique...it had a history. My mind wandered off. Who had worn this ring before me? Definitely a beautiful woman. A flapper? A muse? A princess? And who had given it to her? In my mind's eye, I imagined a dashing French aristocrat getting down on one knee proposing to his stunning true love. While Jaime's eyes remained glued to his *Tribune*, I googled "*toi et moi* ring." I was shocked to read that Napoleon had given one to his fiancée Josephine and that the ring had recently sold at auction for almost one million dollars. Originating in the nineteenth century, the two-stone ring symbolized the eternal union of two souls. Had Jaime known this when he bought the ring? Knowing the issue he had with his father's tragic failed marriage, matrimony couldn't possibly be in his future. There was no doubt in my mind that he feared abandonment—and therefore, commitment. I stole another glance at him. God, that stubbled, blue-eyed face was beautiful. I yearned to turn it my way and sink my lips into his. *Stop it. Gloria!* I silently chided. *This man is lethal. It's all one big game to him.* With a sinking heart, I went back to my e-mails.

Thick silence between us prevailed until we reached Le Bourget. The limo brought us to a special terminal designated for private planes. Wouldn't you know, his private company plane, with the bold orange letters "ZAP!" scrawled across it, was parked next to the hot pink and white Gloria's Secret corporate jet. The sooner I was aboard, the better.

A young ginger-haired steward who I recognized

rushed up to me. "I'm afraid, Ms. Long, I have some bad news."

Now what?

"The maintenance team is reporting engine trouble. They may have to replace a part."

"Engine trouble" were two words I never wanted to hear. My stomach knotted. "How long will that take?" I asked anxiously.

"I've been told it may take up to twenty-four hours."

Fuck. I was stuck in Paris. Though I suppose I could arrange to take a commercial airliner back to Los Angeles. It was just such a long trip—almost twelve hours—and with my fear of flying, it felt more like an eternity. I had no choice. I needed to be back in my office. Infuriated, I whipped out my iPhone and texted our travel department, asking them to find an immediate flight—a non-stop one. The word "layover" was not in my vocabulary. I impatiently waited for a reply and then realized that it was some ungodly hour in the morning in Los Angeles, and my office was still closed. Shit. I was going to have to search for a flight myself. Before I could google Air France, a warm breath curled over the back of my neck.

"Ms. Long."

That velvety, virile voice.

"What?"

"Let me come to the rescue again. I would be honored to have you fly with me on my plane."

Swiveling my head, I stared at him hard as I mulled over his offer. His sparkling blue eyes never strayed from mine.

He playfully tugged at my braid, knowing the

effect that had on me. "The offer expires in thirty seconds. I'm about to board."

"Fine," I huffed back at him.

Damn it. I was going to spend the next twelve hours with this pompous asshole on a plane. With no place to escape.

Chapter 3

J AIME'S PRIVATE PLANE, SOMEWHAT SMALLER than mine, gave me the feeling of being in in someone's modern but comfortable home. The main cabin was outfitted in soft lighting and sleek white leather seating that included an oversized couch and a pair of large reclining chairs that could swivel to face a built-in flat screen monitor. Bright orange pillows and cashmere throws were scattered everywhere. There was also a dining area with a burled table that could accommodate six people as well as a fully stocked bar. Several of his father's colorful abstract paintings lined the shiny white walls.

I sunk into one of the swivel chairs while Jaime plopped down onto the couch opposite me. As much as I hated takeoffs and needed someone's hand to hold on to, I was not going to sit next to him.

"Make yourself at home," Jaime said brightly as we both buckled ourselves in. I noticed that "ZAP!" was engraved into the polished nickel seat belt clasp.

An attractive, mini-skirted brunette came by and offered us drinks. I settled for a glass of white wine hoping it would calm my nerves while Jaime opted for some sparkling water. The attention the attendant lavished on Jaime was not lost on me.

"Enjoy your beverage, Mr. Zander," she said breathily, leaning in close to his lush lips. "And let me know if you need anything else."

The corners of his lips curled up into a sexy smile. "Thanks, Andrea." He kept his eyes on her heart-shaped ass as she sashayed back to the service cabin.

A frisson of jealousy shot through me. Was she one of his many fucks? I wouldn't be surprised. She looked like his type.

"Cheers," said Jaime with an air toast. The wry expression on his face informed me that he had just read my mind.

Cringing, I faked a small smile and took a sip of my wine. The chilled, perfectly balanced liquid went down smoothly. It never ceased to amaze me how even one sip of wine could have such a profound, relaxing effect.

Jaime followed suit with a sip of his water. "So, what do you think?"

"Of your staff?" *Horny bitch!*

"No, of my plane."

I silently huffed. "Your plane's actually very nice."

He grinned that cocky grin. "I designed it so that it would work seamlessly for both my business and personal use."

So for entertaining clients and screwing them. Or having fun with the crew.

"There's a bedroom in the back cabin if you get tired."

I gave him a dirty look. "I don't plan on falling asleep. I have a lot of work to catch up on. I hope you'll respect that."

"I'd be delighted to show you the way if you change your mind."

I rolled my eyes at his words.

Over a loud speaker, the captain told us to prepare for takeoff. My heart dropped to my stomach as the plane whooshed down the tarmac, picking up speed until it lifted off the ground. I squeezed my eyes shut and prayed to God. I just wanted to be in the air cruising smoothly. As the plane made its ascent, my hands balled so hard my fingernails may have drawn blood.

"Are you okay, Ms. Long?" I heard Jaime say.

"Yes," I said through clenched teeth. *Oh God, NO!*

To my shock, I heard my seat belt unfasten, and when I popped my eyes open, I was back in his arms. He quickly transported me to the couch where he sunk down with me in his lap. He secured the orange seat belt around the both of us.

The plane was ascending. I was hyperventilating.

"Relax, Gloria, I've got you."

He was back to calling me Gloria, and I was back to needing him. As the plane continued its climb, I kept my eyes glued shut and leaned my head against his steely chest, his heart beating steadily against me. My breathing calmed. I'd never felt this safe during a takeoff.

When we were finally cruising smoothly, having reached our maximum altitude, my eyes fluttered opened. I tilted my head up, and there he was as if he'd been waiting all this time for me to meet his gaze. His denim blue eyes glistened, and a warm smile played on his gorgeous face. He twisted my long braid around his hand. My core was buzzing.

Damn the effect he was having on me! And even worse, he knew it!

"So, Gloria, is your mind fucking with your body, or is your body fucking with your mind?"

More semantics. "Don't try anything." I spit out the words, unsure if my body's wants were going to trump my mind's commands.

"Hands off. I promise." He raised both hands like someone about to be arrested.

Still sitting on his lap, I suddenly become aware of the warm bulge that was pressing beneath me between my thighs. A bolt of lightening flared through my body.

"Um, uh, I think it's time for me to go back to my seat." I reached for the seat belt clasp, but his hand got there first. He pressed his palm firmly against it, preventing me from undoing it.

"Let me go!" I protested, futilely trying to lift his fingers off the metal fastener. I was seconds away from pounding his chest.

"Look at me, Gloria." It was one of his bossy commands.

Reluctantly, I met his gaze, melting into it. My heart was galloping.

"Why are you afraid of me, Gloria?"

"I'm not afraid of you."

"Bullshit. You've been avoiding me all day."

"I don't want to get hurt," I blurted.

His brows lifted. "Why do you think I'm going to hurt you?"

"I don't want to be thrown into your jar of hearts."

Pensiveness washed over his face. "Meaning..."

"Ending up as one of your fuck'em and leave'em conquests."

He sucked in a gulp of air. "Gloria, you're different. I've told you that. I feel a connection to you that I've never felt with anyone before. Why can't you believe me? Trust me?"

I unconsciously fiddled with his ring. "Because I can't."

"That's not a good enough answer."

Because he rouses feelings in me that I've never felt before. Emotions and sensations that make me lose myself in him. Because he is making me lose control and fall in love. Fighting tears, I murmured, "That's the best I can do."

He released the seat belt and bounced me up with his powerful legs. "Enjoy the rest of your flight."

As I got to my feet, I couldn't help noticing the affronted look on his face. Beneath his steely veneer, there was a layer of vulnerability. As I padded back to my original seat, I glimpsed one of his father's paintings hanging on the cabin wall. It was a self-portrait of a man who looked a lot like Jaime except his eyes were forlorn, missing life-giving highlights. A reminder. Like father like son. His mother had left his father and destroyed him. Like me, Jaime was afraid of being hurt. There was no way in hell a relationship could ever work. On a sigh, my heart grew heavy.

I spent the next couple of hours catching up on e-mails and sales reports, thankful that we were cruising smoothly. Occasionally, I glanced over to Jaime to see what he was doing. He, too, was engrossed in his work, but was also listening to music on his iPod through earphones. His long, jean-clad legs were stretched out along the couch.

He had kicked off his shoes. There was something about his bare, perfectly formed manly feet that was a turn on. My eyes traveled up the length of his muscled limbs, passing over the prominent bulge between his thighs, then across his rippled abs and broad chest, and then on to his gorgeous face. He caught me staring at him, and I immediately turned away. That didn't stop me from gazing at him again. Every so often, our eyes met. It became a game of timing—who could look away faster. It was hard for me to break eye contact with that distracting, sexy, stubbled face. I was losing the game.

About two hours into the flight, a delicious lunch of cold poached salmon over a bed of mixed greens was served by another attractive brunette hostess; she could have easily been the sister of the other attendant, and for all I knew, she was. The image of Jaime fucking them both at the same time flickered in my head. A gaggle of arms and legs, moans and shrieks, cries and sighs. I forced it to go away.

Jaime rose and moved over to the dining table.

"Care to join me, Ms. Long?" he asked before lowering himself to one of the upholstered chairs. A smug smile played on his face.

So, we were back to formalities and smirks.

I quirked a smirk back at him. "I'm fine where I am." I settled the platter on the arm of my chair and watched as the attendant obsequiously served him. I practically choked as she unfolded a napkin and placed it over his crotch and eyed him flirtatiously. Just his type—a shapely brunette who bore a resemblance to Vivien. I was positive beyond reasonable doubt she was one of his many fucks, especially by the way she'd eyed me suspiciously from the moment I'd set foot on the plane. An arrow of jealousy shot through me. And then I coughed up my wine when Jaime said, "Thanks, babe." I felt my face redden and my throat constricting. Luckily, I managed to swallow before choking.

"Are you sure you don't want to join me?" asked Jaime as he lifted his fork to his sensuous mouth. He put a special emphasis on the word "sure" to cajole me. Or should I say, taunt me?

Recovered from nearly gagging, I was tempted to join him at the table, just to piss off that obnoxious, flirty flight attendant, but ultimately I declined. A smug "whatever" expression crossed his face. He shrugged his shoulders and continued to consume his meal, this time without looking my way once. He was playing me for sure, and I didn't like it one bit.

After finishing lunch, I decided I'd done enough work and pulled out my eReader. I had loaded several erotic romance novels onto it before leaving Los Angeles. I'd known that it was unlikely I'd ever get to them with my hectic New York schedule, but now I had an opportunity. Actually, it was more of a need. The need to totally lose myself in a happily ever after fantasy and escape my own uncertain reality and the spell Jaime Zander had on me. He was back on the couch, sprawled out across it, his shoes kicked off, and his eyes closed as he listened to his iPod. I watched as he rhythmically rocked his head and hips to the music that was piping through his earphones. When he began to whistle, I knew what song was making him groove. Gnarls Barkley's "Crazy." Oh, God! Tingles coursed through my body.

My core was aching. This gorgeous man was making *me* crazy. I fought the urge to throw myself on top of him and silence that whistle of his with my mouth. And then really make him crazy. *Stop it, Gloria. Read!*

As I powered on my eReader, the plane suddenly dropped. My stomach did a free fall as a giant lump rose to my throat. The captain's voice filtered through the speaker system. "Mr. Zander and Ms. Long, I'm afraid we have run into some unexpected turbulence."

Turbulence! Nausea spiraled inside me at the sound of the word. The plane shook. And so did my hands. The eReader fell to my lap. I reached for my lunch plate and wine glass to steady them, but not in time. With a shattering crash, they flew to the floor.

"Please be sure your seat belts are securely fastened," the captain continued. I quickly glanced down at mine to be sure it was. My terror-filled eyes then shot over to Jaime. He mumbled "Fuck" as he bolted to an upright position.

To my horror, the plane bounced back up and just as quickly bounced right back down. My stomach rushed to my heart. Everything inside the shaking plane was rattling, especially the bottles inside the liquor cabinet. I glanced outside a window. The wings of the plane were flapping so hard I thought they'd fall off. I gulped. Another bounce!

The unsteadiness of the plane was wrecking havoc on my system. I was petrified. Shaking all over and feeling sick to my stomach. In all my travels, I'd never experienced turbulence as severe as this. The plane continued to yo-yo up and down the sinister gray cloud we were powering through, my torn apart insides bouncing along. Trembling, I squeezed my eyes shut and clutched the armrests, my fingernails clawing the edges. I heard myself hyperventilating as sweat poured out of every crevice of my body. *Deep breath in, deep breath out,* I told myself. It was impossible. My stomach churned. I was going to be sick. Bile pooled in the back of my throat as the plane shook violently, still bouncing across the angry sky. Lunch was on its way up next. Terror consumed me. My frantic pants morphed into frantic whimpers. Tears leaked from my eyes as I cried out loud, "Oh God, oh God, oh God."

My heart was about to beat out of my body. Another major dip. Another shriek. I was going to die! This was it! Maybe I'd faint first! *Please let me faint! Please!* Instinctively, I fumbled for my seat belt—there was no chance in hell it was going to save me—so why the hell was I squeezing it tighter? A set of warm fingers met mine. The clasp snapped open, and in a heartbeat, I was once again in strong, familiar arms, being whisked away. I managed to pry one eye open.

"What are you doing?" The words came out between sobs. "We're going to go down!"

Battling the rocking plane, Jaime staggered down the aisle toward the back of the cabin, holding me tightly. "Angel, if we're going down, we're going together."

"Oh, God!" I shrieked as the plane turned on its side. We both almost went over.

The aircraft straightened, but the turbulence

intensified. Debris was flying all around us. The aircraft's wings flapped madly as they strained against the choppy current. The lights inside the plane flickered, creating the effect of a horror movie of which I was the star.

"Hold on, angel," shouted Jaime as he heaved against the turbulence and protectively shielded me from the debris.

Both eyes squeezed shut again, and the next thing I knew, I was being flung in the air. Thinking I was being catapulted to the land of no return, I crash-landed on my back onto a mattress. Jaime yanked off my leggings and flats, spread my legs, and then crashed on top of me. He maneuvered a wide belt that stretched the width of the bed around us, strapping us in together. I was his prisoner, but I had not the slightest wherewithal to even attempt to fight him. In fact, I welcomed his weight and the belt in my panicked state. As the plane plunged several hundred feet, he fumbled with his jeans zipper and then plunged his cock inside me. I screamed. Not from the extreme drop in altitude but rather from the extreme shock of his sudden penetration.

He growled. "Angel, the only turbulence you're going to feel is the turbulence between your legs." He began to ruthlessly pummel me, my own cockpit responding with a blast of moisture. Whimpering, I wrapped my arms tightly around him, clinging to his hard taut ass. His muscles flexed. As the revved up engine between his legs drove into me, I dug my nails into his raw, hot flesh, the weight of him trampling me against the bed. The plane shook violently. I squeezed my muscles around his powerful cock, an effort to hold on to him even tighter. And to increase the newfound pleasure of this ride from hell.

"Good girl, Gloria. What are you feeling?"

Did he really expect me to speak? I could barely breathe as his cock jettisoned into me. Faster! Harder! Sparing me, he sunk his lips onto mine. I breathed into his mouth, short sharp breaths, as if it were an oxygen bag. As if my life depended on it. The sound of his pounding flesh washed out the rattling of the plane. The air pressure around me dropped as the pressure inside me built. His ruthless pounding took over every fiber of my being. The only turbulence I felt was the turbulence inside me. A tailwind that was spiraling inside me like a tornado. Taking all of me with it. "Stay with me, Angel," Jaime breathed into my ear, his thrusting cock knocking the wind out of me and driving me closer to the edge.

My orgasm was taking off. Just like a jet. Whooshing across the tarmac of my core. Soaring inside me. He was riding me to heaven. Stars swarmed my head. I was flying.

"Gloria, now!" he cried out, as he rocketed to climax. His organ exploded like a meteor, as I crashed around him. Breathing heavy, he buried his head between the soft puffs of clouds that were my breasts. I began to sob. Loud heaving sobs that wracked my body.

"It's okay, angel; it's over now," he said softly. "I've got you." He threaded his fingers through my hair and then smothered my sobs with a deep, passionate kiss. I melted into him.

Our entwined tongues glided smoothly and so

did the plane. We had reached a plateau. I was at last safe with this man, this pilot who could take me under his wings, navigate my body, and then fly me into outer space and make me lose control.

I was floating like a magic carpet. Jaime Zander had conquered my fear of flying. Safe in the harbor of arms, I closed my eyes and let the hum of the plane lull me to sleep.

Chapter 4

"**G**OOD MORNING, EVERYONE. THIS IS your captain. We'll be making our descent into Los Angeles shortly."

Los Angeles? The City of Angels. Had I died and gone to heaven? I peeled my eyes open, one at a time. Sunlight trickled through two small oval windows and made me squint. In my totally disoriented state, it took me a long second to figure out where I was. My eyes spun around the chamber. I was on Jaime's Zander's private plane, half-undressed, in a comfy bed tucked under a duvet with a seat belt secured around my abdomen. I ached everywhere. My chest felt like it had been sledge hammered; my insides felt torn, and my limbs felt bruised. My eyes landed on my black leggings and ballet flats strewn on the carpeted floor. The memories of last night's extreme turbulence and that turbulent fuck with Jaime came crashing at me like a meteorite. Holy, holy fuck! It all felt like a surreal dream.

Jaime Zander's intoxicating scent engulfed me. My eyes darted to the fluffy pillow next to mine. Scrunched up, it had definitely been slept on. But where the hell was he? I bet while I was crashed out, the plane dropped him off in New York. Wait! Did I sleep through a landing and takeoff? Was I really almost in LA? Shit! I'd better get up, showered, and dressed.

I undid the seat belt and pulled my cashmere sweater, the one item of clothing still on my body, up over my head. God was I sore, especially my breasts. As my head re-emerged, the door to the cabin swung open.

"Good morning, angel. Did you sleep well?"

My jaw dropped. It was Jaime! As sinfully sexy as ever. Dressed in a fresh pair of gray sweats that hung dangerously low on his lean hips and his torso bare. My eyes traveled down his perfectly chiseled arms—the arms that had carried me to safety. He was carrying a steaming mug, the tantalizing aroma clearly that of coffee.

I bolted painfully to a sitting position, clutching the duvet to my chest to cover up my now fully naked body. Where I really wanted it was over my head. Mortification raced through my bloodstream. He had seen me at my ultimate worse. A basket case. I was the disaster waiting to happen—not the plane. My sleepy eyes averted the piercing gaze of his beautiful blue eyes. Wearing a cheerful grin, he loped my way.

"I thought you might like some coffee. I had it made just the way you like it—lots of cream."

I greedily grabbed the mug out of his hand and wasted no time putting the steamy contents to my lips. I was in major need of a caffeine fix.

"Hey, don't I get a thank you?"

"Thanks." I flung the word at him with a wrinkle of my nose.

"You're so cute when you make faces."

Inside, I was steaming like the coffee. He was so deliberately exasperating. At least, he didn't want to talk about last night.

After another sip of the delicious brew, it was back to business with this cocky Casanova though my heart was pounding. "What are you still doing here?"

"I have a client to see in Los Angeles."

My insides rattled. The one he called "babe" on the phone?

"And then I thought, I could spend some time with you and get more familiar with your product line."

Fine. As long as he didn't want to get more familiar with me, I was okay with a meeting. I was about to say—"I'll have my assistant Vivien set up something"—but caught myself just in time. I didn't want his venomous stepsister to have anything to do with him. "I'll check my calendar and set up a time. You can come over to our headquarters, and I'll give you a tour."

He smiled sheepishly. "That would be perfect. I'm really looking forward to getting my hands on that new BDSM line of lingerie."

And his hands on me? Stop, it Gloria! I needed to figure out this complicated relationship. The events of last night had set me back. Was I going to let him fuck me as we moved forward? I knew what my mind was thinking and I knew what my body was thinking. For once, couldn't they both agree?

Mulling the future, I continued to sip the delicious coffee. While each sip re-activated my brain, clarity still eluded me. My eyes stayed fixed on his gorgeousness as he ambled over to a closet. When he reappeared, a white tee was folded over a toned arm. I couldn't get my eyes off him as he slipped the tee over his head. His pumped up biceps flexed, and the chiseled muscles of his chest stretched and rippled, that perfect-V elongating and spreading into those washboard abs. I watched, mesmerized, as his sexy, strong-featured face with its layer of dark stubble and crown of tousled chestnut hair emerged through the neck opening. God, why did he have to be so drop dead gorgeous? His gaze met mine as he tucked the tee into his sweats. My core was throbbing, and his cockiness knew it.

"I need to take a shower," I said after a quick final glug of my coffee.

"Make yourself at home. It's over there." He pointed to a door opposite the closet.

Carefully holding the duvet around me like a toga, I slid out of the bed. Under Jaime's smug, watchful gaze, I stood up and took my first steps. For the first time, I discovered how *really* sore I was from that turbulent sex. Every muscle in my body hurt like hell. I felt like I'd been run over by a bulldozer. Slowly and stiffly, I headed toward the bathroom. The stickiness between my legs didn't help.

Jaime broke out into a bellow of laughter.

"Stop it!" I hissed without turning to look back at him. He didn't. My blood was curdling. I was glad he couldn't see my scrunched up face. It was not a pretty picture. I tightened the duvet around me as I continued my walk of shame.

The bathroom was, as I expected, state-of-the art, all creamy rich travertine and brass with high-end fixtures and appliances. An abundant pile of fluffy white and orange towels was stacked on a built-in shelf. Letting the duvet fall to the tiled floor, I stepped into the shower stall after first turning on the water and adjusting the temperature; I deliberately made it extra hot, hoping the steaming water would obliterate my aches. I closed the glass door behind me and positioned myself directly under the showerhead. The powerful hot spray pounded on my aching back, massaging the pain away. Grabbing a large sponge, I put it to my center and washed away the remains of last night. My sensitive folds throbbed beneath my touch. No matter how much I washed, I still felt him inside me. Pulsing, pushing me to the edge. The hum of the plane as it cruised through the air intensified the sensations.

I moved on to the rest of my body. I was shocked by how many bruises were scattered on my torso and my limbs. He had given me fucking, bruising, turbulent sex. Bastard! I hoped he looked for the worse. I was about to find out.

With a yank of the shower door, all six foot three inches of his gorgeous nakedness stepped inside the stall. I gasped.

"What are you doing here?"

He snorted. "What does it look like? I'm taking a shower." He moved in closer to me so that we were face-to-face, sharing the hot, pounding water.

I eyed him from head to foot. There wasn't one bruise on that god-like body. Not a single one!

He reciprocated by giving me the once-over. A maddening, roguish smile spread across his face. "Those are some pretty gnarly bruises."

"You should say you're sorry!"

He arched his brows. "Sorry that I saved your gorgeous ass?"

I clenched my teeth and my fists. Still clutching the sponge, I wanted to slap him with it. Before I could, he grabbed it out of my hand.

Gently, he circled it around each breast. I could feel my sensitive nipples pucker, sending the tingling sensation of arousal once again to my core. My breathing grew shallow.

I sucked in air between my teeth. "Stop it!"

Still washing my tender breasts, he leaned into me, strands of his drenched hair falling into his hooded eyes. "Come on, you don't really want me to stop, Gloria."

He was right. I stood paralyzed as the sparks inside me intensified. I could feel his erection pressing against my middle. He was turning himself on as he turned me on.

"I'm sorry about the bruises, angel." There was genuine regret in his voice. "But no imperfections can mar your beauty...not even this one."

I stiffened as he bent over and tenderly kissed my scar. The scar I wished I could rip off my body and throw away with the memories it held.

He released his mouth and his eyes lifted to mine. "It's from a gunshot, isn't it, Gloria?" I quivered as he ran his fingers gently over the shiny, raised flesh. It no longer had any feeling, but the ache it left in my heart never went away.

The spray of the shower cascaded over us like a summer thunderstorm. A bolt of lightening flashed through me, searing my nerves. "How do you know that?"

His eyes grew murky blue with pain. "My father. Remember, he put a gun to his head. I'm the one who found him. I'll never forget what that bullet hole looked like. Never."

"I'm sorry," I murmured. I genuinely was. No child should have to endure that tragedy. Filled with both shame and sadness, I bowed my head. My eyes gazed down at the hideous scar just above my left breast. His long index finger continued to rub it gently.

"It almost pierced your heart, didn't it?"

I said nothing. Emotionally, it did pierce my heart. The hole it left deep inside my soul had never closed up. Madame Paulette's words rang in my ears. *"Ma chérie*, the scars that you don't see are *zee* hardest to heal."

Finally, I broke my silence. "I don't want to talk about it. It has to do with something in my past that I'm trying to leave behind." Tears threatened to spill from my eyes.

"Ah, the past that makes you who you are, Gloria. The past that you must let go of to move forward."

His profound, insightful words tugged at my heartstrings. I hoped there'd come a day when I could close the door on my past but knew that was wishful thinking. It took all I had not to cry. I bit down on my quivering lip.

He gently tilted up my chin with his other hand. I met his soulful eyes—the eyes he rarely exposed but I loved most. I lost control. Tears escaped my eyes and mingled with the spray of the shower.

He tenderly brushed them away with the pads of this thumbs. "You're crying, aren't you?"

With a sniffle, I nodded. "I'm sorry. It's just too painful to go there."

"We all have our secrets, Gloria. Even I have mine. When you trust me with yours, I know your heart will be mine."

I fidgeted with his exquisite *toi et moi* ring, trying to make sense of his words. Before I could ask what he meant, the captain's muffled voice sounded in my ears.

"Mr. Zander and Ms. Long, we will be beginning our descent into Van Nuys Airport. Please return to your seats and make sure your seat belts are securely fastened."

As I took a step toward the shower door, Jaime grabbed me by the elbow. In one smooth move, he spun me around and smashed his lips onto mine. The kiss was deep, passionate, and bruising. My mouth and my body sunk into it. I wrapped my arms around his broad shoulders, my wet velvet breasts rubbing against his sculpted pecs. His powerful erection pressed against my middle as I felt a thick long finger slide across my cleft. He ran circles around my clit, turning it into a hard nub and sending a current of pleasure to my core.

"Come on, Gloria. We have time for a quick fuck."

"I don't think so," I said as I felt the plane descending.

It was too late. His hands had already parted my legs, making room for his slick, rigid length to penetrate me. I was still sore from last night's rough encounter, but once he was in, my inner muscles relaxed and I was able to take him to the hilt. I moaned with ecstasy.

"Oh, angel, you're incredible," he breathed into my ear. His finger continued to work my clit as he pounded furiously. I clutched his shoulders for support while he cinched my waist with his free hand. My head arched, my eyes squeezed shut, and my mouth formed an "O." Droplets of water fell onto my tongue. I undulated my hips, meeting his every mighty thrust. Grunting, he accelerated his pace, grinding harder and faster with single-minded fury. I felt like an airplane, going down, spiraling out of control. But I wasn't afraid of crashing. I wanted to explode. Badly.

"Fall apart, now!" he commanded.

On his words, I broke into a million pieces. I screamed so loud I thought an attendant might hear us. Jaime shouted my name and shattered inside me, showering me with his own release.

We just stood there, forehead to forehead, our cloaked eyes just a palm's width apart as the powerful shower beat down upon us. Slowly, he withdrew his cock.

"Come on, Ms. Long, it's time to prepare for landing." He took my hand in his and led me out of the shower.

As he wrapped a big fluffy white bath towel around me, I berated myself. Why hadn't I resisted him?

Because he was too strong, too determined, too beautiful.

And because I was hopelessly, helplessly head over heels in love.

Chapter 5

"**D**O YOU WANT TO HOLD my hand?" crooned Jaime as the plane began its final descent into Los Angeles. I detected mockery in his voice. It so irritated me how fast he could go back to being so cocky and annoying.

"No," I snapped back at him. I was surprisingly relaxed though it was comforting to be seated next to him on the couch in the main cabin. My seat belt was fastened securely around me.

I gazed out one of the aircraft's windows. Below, the familiar trafficked intertwining freeways, the cars resembling crawling bugs, and rows of red-roofed Spanish cottages came into view. I flashbacked to the first time I had flown to Los Angeles with Kevin. We had arrived at LAX in the early evening, dusk. I was still so weak from the bullet hole Boris Borofsky had bore into my chest and suffering from airsickness. But when all the twinkly lights came into view, my spirits lifted. The City of Angels. The City of Dreams. Clutching Kevin as we waited for a cab outside the terminal, I gazed in awe at the pink-streaked sky, tall palms, and multi-color flowers. I was shocked that it was so warm when it was mid-December. The cold, gray winter of Brighton Beach was now miles away. And so was the pink-eyed monster. The horror of that one regrettable night was behind us. There was a chance for a new beginning in this fairy-tale city where dreams could come true.

While I was remarkably fearless as Jaime's plane streamlined to the ground, a mental sigh of relief sang inside me as it touched down at Van Nuys Airport. Once it came to a complete halt, the flight attendants ushered us off. The two attractive brunettes flirtatiously bid Jaime good-bye but still regarded me with unfriendly, suspicious eyes.

Van Nuys Airport was a small airport located in what was known in LA as "The Valley." It was a hub for corporate jets and private planes, allowing wealthy business commuters and celebrities the opportunity to avoid the hassle of getting in and out of busy LAX, Los Angeles's main airport.

I checked my iPhone. It was a little after 1:00 p.m. PST, and the weather was SoCal perfect—sunny, mid seventies, not a cloud in the sky. My west coast driver, Tyrone Turrell—Ty, for short—greeted me on the tarmac with my corporate car which happened to be a black Range Rover just like the one Jaime used to get chauffeured around in New York. Ty was a twenty-one-year-old handsome black man with a brick shithouse build whom I'd rescued from South Central's drug and crime-ridden streets. After being released from prison for a gang-related crime, he was recruited at the age of eighteen to serve in a remedial apprenticeship program for troubled street kids. It had turned him around and made him into one of the finest young men I knew. With my own challenging childhood, I was a big believer in giving back and helping disadvantaged youth. In fact, later in the week, I was being honored with a Lifetime Achievement Award for the work I'd done for Girls Like Us, the charitable organization that I'd founded and supported ardently.

"Welcome back, Ms. Long," Ty said with a big toothy smile and a tip of his driver's hat. "Sorry to hear you had engine trouble." He eyed Jaime, who was standing beside me. "Who may be your gentleman friend?"

Jaime introduced himself before I could utter a word and then shook Ty's massive hand. "I'll be working with Ms. Long on the new Gloria's Secret ad campaign."

Ty gave Jaime his seal of approval by making a circle with his thumb and forefinger. "Ms. Long's got mighty fine taste."

My face flushed with embarrassment.

Jaime glanced my way, amused by my heated expression. "I'd have to agree with that." I swear he was mentally undressing me. Nerve-zapping tingles raced up and down my body.

"Um, uh, where are you staying?" I asked Mr. Distracting.

"I always stay at Shutters."

Shutters On the Beach in Santa Monica was one of my favorite hotels. With its gray-shingled design, it reminded me of a charming New England hotel, and the service was impeccable. I often had out-of-town vendors and store managers stay there, meeting them sometimes for breakfast or drinks. The oceanfront location with its view of the pier was spectacular. I was surprised I'd never encountered Jaime there. Timing, I'd learned as a businesswoman, was everything. If you waited too long or acted too soon, everything could change... for better or for worse.

"Do you have a means of transportation?" I asked my companion.

"Actually, I was hoping you could give me a ride. I'll pick up a car at the hotel."

I hesitated then agreed. I just wasn't sure how much more time I could spend with him in a confined means of transportation. I'm sure he wouldn't try anything with Ty in the car. But then again...

Ty loaded our luggage onto a dolly. Jaime had one piece—a small roll away bag— and I had, well... many.

Jaime rolled his eyes at my mountain of luggage. "Sheesh, angel. You pack like there's no tomorrow."

My breath hitched. Not because of his snarky comment but because he'd called me "angel" in front of Ty. The wide-eyed expression on my driver's face told me the reference was not lost on him. Clearing my throat, I said, "It's not just my wardrobe. There are lots of last minute samples from the Gloria's Secret line that I had to transport to New York for the fashion show."

"I look forward to seeing them again," Jaime said with a wink. "Perhaps you'll model them for me."

My eyes shot him daggers. I pressed my lips tight as I followed Ty, with Jaime beside me, to the car. While the hot shower had helped soothe my bruised body, my stride was still stiff.

Ty cranked his head to check on me. "You're walking a little funny, Ms. Long. Are you okay?"

Jaime jumped in. "She had a hard workout. She's just not used to it."

Cringing, I fired him a I'm-going-to-kill-you look. The sparks were flying.

I heard Ty murmur, "Oh my."

Jaime was back to whistling "Crazy." Let me at him!

"Stop whistling!" I barked at him.

Jaime continued as if he had deaf ears. He was so damn deliberately irritating.

Tyrone joined in, swinging his head and hips rhythmically, as he did his finest impression of Gnarls Barkley. I blew out a loud puff of air. *Men!*

Inside the car, things calmed down. To my relief, Jaime behaved and sat his distance in the back seat.

"How long have you lived in LA?" he asked as the car turned onto the southbound 405 Freeway.

"Fifteen years."

"What brought you here?"

"Work," I lied. *Desperation. Fear. Hope.* Kevin and I had managed to escape New York just in time... before Boris Borofsky could track us down with his army of Russian mafia.

"Did you leave family behind?"

"Just one special woman." The image of Madame Paulette filled my head. It still seemed unreal that she was gone. Her burial in Paris seemed so distant.

"Oh, your mother?"

I inwardly shuddered. I didn't want to talk about my crack whore mother or my neglected, tormented childhood.

Jaime's cell phone rang, sparing me from responding. He pulled the phone out of his jeans pocket and furrowed his brows when he viewed the caller ID. My eyes skimmed over it. It read "Blocked Caller ID." It rang again.

"Fuck. I've got to take this. It's important." His jaw tensed when he hit answer. He put the phone to his ear and listened intensely. The words that came out of his mouth were cryptic like... "yes"..."no"... "can't talk right now"... "will call you later"... "trust me." He terminated the call and nervously tapped the phone on his muscular thigh.

Trust me? I cringed at the words. How many times had I heard it? Was that what he said to all his fucks? It was her. His other client—the one he called "babe." He was definitely hiding something from me.

It was my turn to test him. I inhaled deeply. "Do you want to have dinner tonight? We can talk about the budget for the advertising campaign."

Jaime frowned. "I can't. I've got another commitment."

I knew he was lying because he couldn't look me straight in the eyes. My heart sunk to my stomach. There was no doubt in my mind—the rogue was fucking someone else tonight. It was his "other" client or one of those flirty flight attendants; he called them "babe" too. I regretted that I'd boldly asked him out.

"No problem." My voice wavered. "Maybe you can come by the office tomorrow around two. I'll show you around."

He checked his iPhone calendar. "Two-ish. That we would be good."

We spent the rest of the ride steeped in silence.

His face remained tense. He was definitely covering up something. I diverted my attention by checking my e-mails and texts. There were over a dozen from Kevin. All of them said the same thing: *URGENT! CALL ME ASAP!*

It was unlike Kevin to use shouty caps. Something was definitely wrong. I was tempted to call Kevin right away. But I didn't want to have a conversation with him in front of Jaime. I had a gut feeling that it involved his assistant Ray, and the last thing I wanted to do was let Jaime know that there was—or had been—something going on between the two of them. My eyes flitted to Jaime, whose face remained impassive. He was gazing out the window, and from his furrowed brows, I could tell his mind was elsewhere. He was ignoring me, as if I didn't exist. As if the last few days didn't exist. I was like a stranger to him. I gazed down at the twinkling *toi et moi* ring and twisted it around my finger so that the diamonds didn't glare in my face. Suddenly, I remembered that I had left something behind in Paris. My heart.

The early afternoon traffic on the 405 was fortunately moderate. I instructed Ty to make a stop at my place first before dropping Jaime off at Shutters. Located on the famed Wilshire Corridor in Westwood, my condo was just a few exits before the 10 Freeway which led into Santa Monica. I needed to get away from Jaime as quickly as possible. I was suffocating sharing the same air as him.

Ty pulled into the circular driveway of the majestic

high-rise building I lived in. It was considered the swankiest building on the Corridor, the condos going in the millions. Numerous celebrities lived in the building although I was the lucky one who inhabited the spacious penthouse apartment. Kevin lived one floor below me, in an equally stunning apartment. Our current abodes were a far cry from the small two-bedroom apartment we shared in the Hollywood Hills when we first started out in LA. Unfortunately, Victor Holden lived there too. I wondered if Jaime knew.

Ty jumped out of the car and opened my passenger door. He immediately began to unload my baggage from the trunk. I had one foot out the door when Jaime grabbed me by the elbow.

"Let go of me, please." My voice was as cold as dry ice.

"Hey, aren't you even to going to say good-bye?"

Before I could say a word, he spun me around and smacked a bruising kiss on my lips.

Damn! What his lips could do to me! My temperature rose, and my heart hammered, not knowing whether to give in to him or resist him. I called upon all the mind control I could muster and broke away.

I turned my head away from him, avoiding eye contact. "Please, I've got to go."

Tightening his grip on my elbow with one hand, he fisted my long braid with the other, yanking it hard until I was forced to face him. Our eyes connected. His stubbled, swoon-worthy face melted me. His blue eyes bore a hole in each of my mismatched ones.

"Gloria, I really enjoyed sharing Paris with you." His voice was soft and breathy.

An avalanche of memories bombarded my head. The bath...the Louvre...the roses...the Ferris wheel... the ring. *Toi et moi*. My aching heart sank to my stomach. Words stayed trapped in my throat, but tears were brewing. I inhaled a deep breath to keep them from falling.

Jaime sensed my distress. The look on his face became one of confusion and concern. He brushed the tip of my braid across my chin. "What's the matter, angel?"

Calling me "angel" again almost put me over the edge. *Keep it together, Gloria. Don't let this man make you fall apart*, my logic pleaded.

"I'm just tired...that's all." I was actually worn out by this man. By the way he could play with my body, my mind, and my fragile heart and tear them all apart.

I finally jerked away and leaped out of the car.

"Gloria, wait!"

"Have fun tonight," I managed through clenched teeth.

"Gloria, it's not... "

What you think. I'd heard these words once too many times and was over that lame excuse. Cutting him off, I slammed the heavy door shut and sprinted past the doorman into my building. Ty was waiting for me in the elegantly appointed lobby with my luggage piled high on a dolly. I surveyed the statuesque man with the build of Mr. Clean. He could easily trample Jaime if he came after me.

I hurried to the elevator, almost running. I glanced over my shoulder to see if Jaime had followed me into the building. He hadn't. I would be lying to say I was grateful.

With my palm, I anxiously pounded the "UP" call button. To my relief, the doors parted instantly and so did my mouth. Looming before me was Victor Holden. He was clad in an expensive equestrian outfit—a navy riding jacket, tight cream britches, and shiny leather boots. Under one arm was a black velvet helmet and dangling from the hand of the other was a worn leather riding crop. The sight of the latter made me inwardly shudder. Was this the riding crop he'd beaten Jaime with as a child? While I'd seen Victor in this uniform before, it now revolted and enraged me knowing his history of physical abuse.

His steel-gray eyes, like needles, pierced mine. "Gloria," he sneered.

"Hello, Victor," I said icily. Avoiding his gaze, I stepped into the elevator, expecting him to step out. Except he didn't. The doors slid closed, and I was trapped inside with him. The memory of his repulsive sexual assault in Paris flooded my head. Jaime had rescued me, but there was no Jaime Zander in sight now.

Anxiously, I reached for the "Open Door" button to escape. Before I could make contact with it, Victor caught my wrist and, in one coordinated move, slammed me hard against the side wall. He pressed his hard-as-nails body against me, painfully crushing my own bruised body. The remains of his lunchtime bourbon lingered on his breath and nauseated me. I squirmed, trying to free myself from his weight, but I was no match for his strength. The man, despite his age, regularly worked out with a trainer in addition to being an accomplished equestrian and was more fit than someone half his age. The elevator remained stagnant. The air thickened. My pulse rate quickened.

He leaned in to me, his stinking breath heating my face. "I don't pay you two million dollars a year and a hefty bonus to fuck your brains out with that Zander piece of shit in Paris."

Despite my shallow breathing, I held my own and looked straight into his eyes. "I was there on personal business, and I also met with Sandrine, the General Manager of the Champs-Elysées store."

His lips snarled. "Don't bullshit me, Gloria. I'm not a patient man."

My eyes stayed lock on his. Though my heart was racing, I was not going to let him intimidate me. "I know why you hate him." *And why he hates you.* My body contorted with fury at the thought of him physically abusing young Jaime.

His face grew glacial. "It doesn't matter why I hate him. What disturbs me more than his relationship with Gloria's Secret is his personal relationship with you. This is no time to be fucking your brains out. In case you didn't know, while you were getting it on in Paris, there was a big sell off this morning of Gloria's Secret stock. The stock plunged twenty points. Your job is on the line. There's a lot of speculation that you'll be out on your sweet ass soon."

My stomach knotted up. How was that possible? By all Wall Street estimates, our earnings were solid and our forecast healthy. In fact, before the long weekend, the stock had closed at an all time high, and many analysts had put Gloria's Secret stock on their "Buy now" list, expecting further growth. Kevin's "urgent" e-mails flashed into my head— the stock crisis, that's what they must have been about.

Victor's sinister eyes bore into mine. "I'm not

going to save your precious ass, Gloria, unless you give me what I want."

My blood simmered. He was threatening me. His body pressed harder against mine, his repulsive erection pulsing against my middle. My eyes clashed with his. "I don't have to give you anything, Victor, except my commitment to the growth of Gloria's Secret. This is harassment."

"You don't know what harassment is. Let me show you." Allowing his helmet to tumble onto the polished marble floor, he lifted his right hand to my face and pinched a cheek. With the other, he poked my clit with the handle of his riding crop.

I winced. "Let go of me, Victor. You're hurting me."

He poked my clit again and then moved his slimy lips closer to mine. Before they could touch down, the elevator doors parted. Startled, he released me. He quickly picked up his helmet and straightened his riding jacket.

Confession: So much of me wanted to see Jaime standing before me. The fantasy of him grabbing Victor's riding crop and striking him with it played in my head. Giving the fuckwad what he deserved.

It was Tyrone with my luggage. Though wishing it had been Jaime, I inwardly sighed with relief. My pulse rate remained accelerated. I was still reeling from Victor's vicious assault and threat.

Tyrone was a six foot seven hunk of a man that, trust me, you didn't want to mess with. With a contemptuous huff, Victor stiffly headed out the elevator. As the doors began to close, he struck his riding crop against one of them, forcing them to open again.

"Have a nice day, Gloria, and think about my offer or Tyrone may be out of a job too." His chilly voice matched his demeanor as he strode into the lobby.

The whites of Tyrone's eyes popped. "Waz that man talking about?"

It was no secret that Tyrone despised Victor. Why not? The arrogant Chairman of the Board looked down upon him and had once even told him to his face that he should go back to the ghetto streets from where he'd come. I'd literally had to jump between them so that Ty didn't physically take Victor down. The violent streak in Tyrone was something to be feared.

"Nothing, Ty."

Tyrone, no dummy, could see I was visibly shaken as I pressed the button for my penthouse. My fingers were jittery. "You okay, Ms. Long?"

I nodded. "Yes, thank you." Truthfully, as the doors slid closed again and the elevator made its ascent, I felt like the ground was opening beneath me, and I was falling into a deep abyss.

Jaime Zander had fucked with my heart enough in the last forty-eight hours, and now I had to contend with his vicious stepfather Victor and the possibility that I was going to lose everything I had built. The truth was hard to face. I swallowed hard past the painful lump in my throat.

Usually after a long business trip, I found comfort being back home. My spacious, two-story sunlit apartment had been elegantly furnished in an all white and gilt Hollywood Regency style by one of Los Angeles's top interior designers, and it had views of Los Angeles from all sides. From the many windows, I could see downtown skyscrapers, the majestic mansion-dotted Hollywood Hills, and the sparkling Pacific Ocean. The spectacular panoramic view usually brought me peacefulness, but today it did nothing to alleviate the sick sinking feeling in both my heart and stomach.

After Ty took my luggage upstairs and departed, I immediately tried calling Kevin. No answer. He must have been on ten phones at once putting out fires. I left him a message to call me back ASAP.

With my cell phone in one hand and my handbag in the other, I trudged up the stately winding stairs to my bedroom and collapsed onto my sumptuous four-poster bed. Outstretched on my thick duvet, I stared blankly at the high ceiling. My stomach twisted with nerves, and my heart beat a mile a minute. I couldn't think straight. My head was pounding. Was my job really on the line? Was I going to have to give in to Victor's lascivious demands to save myself and the company I'd built from the ground up? I closed my eyes and dug holes into my temples with my index fingers, hoping to numb the pain and get some clarity. It was futile. I was close to hyperventilating. *Breathe, Gloria, breathe. Inhale. Exhale.* I did it again and again and again. Finally, the deep breathing exercise kicked in, and my torrent of emotions settled. I snapped my eyes open and glanced at the alarm clock on my night table. 2:30 p.m.

"*C'est la guerre,*" Madame Paulette had often said

when things got rough. The strength of this amazing women seeped into my veins. Yes, this was war, but I had faced worse battles before. The memory of Boris Borofsky holding a gun to my chest flashed in and out of my head. I had stared death in the face and beat it.

Propping myself up on my elbows, I reached for my cell phone and dialed the front desk.

"Can you please bring my car around," I asked the building attendant. I was going to drive myself to my office and find out first-hand what was going on.

I jumped out of the bed and quickly shed my leggings uniform. I ambled over to my hand-painted lingerie chest and rifled through it until I found what I was looking for. They were not hard to find: my cherry red lace push up bra with the front bow closing, matching thong, and garter. From the drawer below, I pulled out a fresh pair of black sheer silk stockings. I scrambled to put on the undergarments and then sat back down on the bed to slip on the stockings. I gingerly rolled them up over my bruised legs and clipped them to the bow-tipped garters. My legs went from being mush to steel.

I then paraded into my walk-in closet and yanked one of my favorite power suits off a hanger—my red bouclé Chanel. Red, the color of fire and blood. The color of power. I quickly slipped it on. I then scoured my Louis Vuitton travel trunk for the pair of shoes I was seeking. I found them quickly—spiky black patent pumps with killer red soles—the Louboutins I'd worn to the ZAP! pitch. I slipped them onto my feet and suddenly I was six inches taller. Jaime had called them my "fuck me" shoes. I had a new name for them—*fuck you* shoes.

I had set my priorities straight. Fuck Jaime. Fuck Victor. What mattered most was the future of everything I'd worked for. Gloria's Secret. I was not going to let any man make me—or my empire—fall apart.

I quickly re-braided my hair and applied my favorite red lipstick. I was back to being in control.

Chapter 6

THE DRIVE FROM MY CONDO to my office took fifteen minutes. It was located in Culver City. Occupying the lot of a former movie studio, it was a compound consisting of executive offices, a design studio, and a manufacturing plant. I was proud to say that all Gloria's Secret garments were made with love in America. And I equally prided myself on the high company morale. Employees were paid fairly and received excellent benefits, including childcare and opportunities to further their education. I never forgot my roots and felt obliged to give back.

Passing through gated security, I drove my black hardtop Porsche into the parking lot and pulled it into the spot reserved for me. My name "Gloria" with our signature pink heart beneath it was scrawled on the reserved parking sign; it always brought a big smile to my face. I had worked hard for this spot and no one, especially Victor Holden, was going to take it away from me. To my relief, Kevin's car, a cute leafy green Fiat convertible, was parked next to mine. I couldn't wait to see him and hear his take on what was going on.

Holding my purse in one hand and my briefcase in the other, I marched into the sprawling two-story building that housed my office. Madame Paulette had always said, "Form equals meaning." With that in mind, I had designed the interior of our main office building to reflect our brand. It was whimsical, sexy, and feminine. The feeling of a boudoir. Sleek white leather couches sat on zebra-patterned rug and were surrounded by framed poster-size covers of various Gloria's Secret catalogues on the walls. The receptionist sat behind a massive shiny white Formica elliptical console that bore a colossal vase of fragrant hot pink roses. The Gloria's Secret logo with its insignia hot pink heart was plastered on the wall behind her. Claudia, the lovely redheaded Latino receptionist who I'd mentored through my Girls Like Us program, had her face buried in her computer.

"Good afternoon, Claudia," I said.

Startled, the young, pretty receptionist looked up from her computer with a gasp. "Gloria!"

Her wide eyes told me she was surprised to see me. I hadn't told anyone, even Kevin, that I was returning to the office today.

"Are you okay?" Her face was tensed up and her voice wavered.

The beginnings of rage coursed through my blood. Did even the receptionist know about the stock crisis and my uncertain future with the company? Damn it! I bet everyone knew. I took a deep breath and steeled myself. "Yes, Claudia. Everything's just fine." I forced a small smile and stomped down the long hallway to my office. I cursed Victor Holden every heel-clicking step of the way. *Fuck him! Yes, fuck him!*

Nervous hellos accompanied by nervous faces

bombarded me as I marched through the corridor. My façade was cheerful but inside I was cringing. Yes, everyone knew!

When I got to my corner suite, I expected to see Vivien sitting outside my office at her desk. Her desk instead was vacant, but truthfully, I was relieved. I despised the little vixen, who'd seduced Jaime Zander, almost as much as I despised her father. Just like him, she was ruthless, crafty, and vindictive. A diabolical dominatrix. She was not to be trusted. Not one bit.

I surmised she must be in the restroom. She made it a habit of primping herself before a mirror several times a day. Often, she would be away from her desk for long stretches of time. Once, almost an hour. I'd caught her trying on new clothes and ordered her back to her desk. She completely ignored me. She was the Chairman of the Board's daughter and knew she could get away with it. And there was no way I could fire her.

The shock of the stock crash and my impending doom was nothing compared to the shock I got when I stepped foot inside my spacious crystal chandelier-lit office, a slightly smaller version of the lobby. I froze. Seated in my hot pink velvet swivel chair behind my white lacquered desk was Vivien. Her eyes clashed with mine. A raging fire surged inside me.

"What are you doing at my desk?"

A poisonous smile slithered across her face. "Daddy told me that you may be on your way out. I was just trying your desk out for size."

My eyes narrowed into blades of steel. "I'm not

going anywhere. Now, get the fuck out of my chair!"

Not wiping off her wicked smirk, she slowly stood up. She was wearing a so very-Vivien purple knit mini dress that clenched her curvy body and accentuated her globe-sized fake boobs.

"You know, Gloria, you shouldn't treat your employees so rudely. Isn't there some kind of company policy forbidding lewd language? You're just lucky I'm not going to go to human resources and report you for harassment."

I could actually visualize puffs of smoke blowing out of my nostrils. Clenching my fists, I kept my eyes on her as she sauntered out of my office. At the doorway, she paused and pivoted her head. "By the way, Gloria, I forgot to ask you. How was Paris with Jaime? I hear that may be over soon too."

I could feel my face reddening with rage. How the hell did she know what was going on with Jaime and me? Even Victor didn't know the extent of our relationship. And why was she so sure it was coming to an end? I bit down hard-on my lip to stifle a snake-tongued retort and clenched my fists tighter so that I wouldn't throw something at her. Or strangle her.

"Please send me the latest sales reports when you get back to your desk," I finally managed through gritted teeth. "And close the door behind you."

"No problem," she replied snidely. On her way out, she slammed the door shut.

Inhaling a gulp of air, I sat down at my desk. The cloying scent of Vivien lingered in the air and nauseated me. I immediately got to work and responded to the influx of e-mails that were facing me on my large state-of-the-art computer screen. Right after I responded to a meeting with one of our fabric vendors, an e-mail from Sales with the most recent Excel sales reports attached came through. My heart pounded. I wasted no time opening the attachments and perusing them.

By the time I got to the fifth report, my nerves calmed down. Sales were as steady as always. In fact, U.S. and international sales were stronger than ever. I was now more befuddled than anxious. What could be causing so many to sell off the stock and causing the price of shares to plummet? I needed to do more research—find out what investors had bailed. I shot off an urgent e-mail to Finance to compile a list.

"Glorious!"

My door swung open and my eyes looked up. Kevin.

"Why didn't you let me know you were coming into the office?" Wearing stylish shorts and high tops, he jogged over to me, and we hugged. God, did I need a big dose of Kevin!

I perched my left elbow on my desk and wearily sunk my chin into my palm while Kevin plunked down into one of the two pink and white striped armchairs positioned in front of my desk. My right hand rested on my lap beneath my desk.

I didn't know where to begin. "Oh, Kev, it's been just a fucking nightmare since I got back from Paris."

"Tell me about it. I've been on rumor control all day. My phones haven't stopped ringing. I'm sorry couldn't get back to you." He paused. "I've got bad news."

My eyes widened with a skip of my heartbeat. *Now what?*

His expression turned somber. "The *New York Times* is going to run a front-page story in the Business Section tomorrow about our stock sell off. The headline: *Gloria's Secret CEO Rumored to Exit as Stock Plummets.*

"Fuck!" I banged my desk with my left fist.

Kevin lowered his long-lashed hazel eyes and nervously twisted his diamond stud earring. "I'm sorry, Glorious. I couldn't stop them."

I despondently shook my head. "Kev, it's not your fault. But I just don't get it. There's no reason for investors to be jittery. I just reviewed our sales reports and forecasts, and they're all solid. And with our new BDSM-inspired line and the launch of our sex toys, we should be golden."

Kevin looked up and met my pensive eyes. "I'm as surprised as you are. But one thing's for sure, if you're leaving, I'm leaving with you."

I rose and came around my desk to give him another great big hug. "I love you, Kev."

"Right back at you, Glorious."

I plopped down on my desk, crossing my legs and placing my hands under my butt. Kev and I had been through so much together. If it hadn't been for him, there would be no Gloria's Secret. I owed him my career and my life. There was no one I trusted more than Kevin. Or loved. Except...

Kevin cut my thoughts short. "So, tell me something good. How was Paris?"

My shoulders heaved on a loud sigh. The only

good thing about the stock crisis was that it had kept my mind off Jaime. But at the mention of Paris, all the dreamy memories came racing back into my head.

"Oh, Kev, it was fucking amazing."

Kevin's face brightened. "Don't hold back. Tell me everything."

Kevin was the one person I confided in completely. Like a broken record, I relayed everything that had happened there beginning with Madame Paulette's dignified funeral, my encounter with Victor, and Jaime's rescue.

"Victor's a fucking douchebag," Kevin grumbled.

"It gets worse and more complicated." I proceeded to share Jaime's past and the knowledge that Victor was Jaime's abusive stepfather and that Vivien had seduced him when he was a teenager.

Kevin's eyes widened. "This is like a bad soap opera."

Continuing, I told Kevin about the Ferris wheel ride and then about our turbulent plane ride home.

"Get out! That's so fucking off the fuck charts. I mean like a hundred on a scale of one to ten."

I laughed—something I so needed to do. And then my expression morphed from cheerfulness back to gloom. Tears stormed my eyes.

"What's the matter, Glorious? Everything with Jaime sounds so fan-fucking-tastic."

My right hand came out from under my butt to wipe away a tear that had escaped. Kevin batted his eyes in shock.

"Glorious, what's that on your middle finger?"

"It's a *toi et moi* ring." I paused, having deliberately

omitted this detail, and then sighed. "Jaime gave it to me on the Ferris wheel."

Kevin grasped my hand and examined the brilliant double diamond ring close up. "Holy shit! This man is seriously in love with you."

The floodgates broke loose; a tsunami of tears rushed down my face. "No, Kev. He's not. I'm just another one of his many fucks. He was really devastated by his father's suicide after his mother left him for Victor. He has serious commitment issues."

"I don't believe that. No man gives a ring like this to someone he doesn't care about."

"Trust me, he's not that into me. He even has a date with someone else tonight."

Kevin furrowed his brows. "Are you sure about that?"

"Positive. When I asked him if he wanted to have dinner with me, he told me he had a previous commitment. And right before we left Paris, I overheard him on his cell tell someone he called 'babe' that he'd hook up with her as soon as he got to LA."

"That sucks big time." Kevin brushed away my tears. He was one of the few people I didn't feel embarrassed crying in front of. He had seen me shed many tears over my lifetime.

My sobs subsided a little. "Kev, thanks for listening. I've talked way too much about myself. What about you? What's going on?"

He let out a girlish sigh. "Nothing good. Jaime's assistant Ray was a great fuck, but it turns out he's in a relationship."

"Oh, I'm so sorry." I truly was. Kevin never had

any luck in the boyfriend department. Life was just so unfair. I gave my dear friend a peck on the cheek. "Ray doesn't know what he's missing out on." My Kev tweaked a smile.

"Glorious, I've got to get back to work. There's still a lot of fires to put out."

Nodding, I smiled back at him. "Let me know if there's anything you need from me." A warm feeling radiated inside me. I was so blessed to have Kevin in my life.

"Hey, what are you up to tonight?" he asked at the doorway before exiting my office.

"Nothing."

A grin lit up his face. "Then you're invited to a Pity Party for Two at my place."

"Can't wait!" My lips curled into a smile. I had something to look forward to. Kev and I had celebrated—or should I say, moped—together this way before. It meant pigging out on pepperoni pizza, a bottle or two or more of wine, a gallon of Haagen-Dazs vanilla ice cream... and sometimes a good cry. This deadly combination was a panacea for all troubles, no matter how big or small. It was, before Jaime came into my life, the only way I ever let myself lose control.

After Kevin went back to his office to deal with our stock nightmare —I'm sure the *Wall Street Journal* among other business periodicals would be breaking the story too—I continued to study the sales reports and forecasts. I focused hard, forcing Jaime out of my mind every time he snuck into it. After carefully reviewing all of the material, I still couldn't find anything out of the ordinary. I was more perplexed than ever about the sudden sell off. Was I missing something? A ping on my computer signaling a new e-mail diverted my attention. It was from Lou Bartone in Finance...responding to my inquiry. I immediately opened it. As I read it, my eyes grew wide. Victor Holden had been among the early shareholders who had traded in the stock. Fifty thousand shares to be exact, I recognized several other names on the list—most were close business associates of Victor's. A mixture of rage and confusion consumed me. Was Victor playing dirty? Was he deliberately trying to bring me down? With an angry jab of my finger, I forwarded Lou's e-mail to him. Above the list of investor names, I typed: *Can you please explain?* What I really wanted to write was: *What the fuck?*

I stared anxiously at my computer screen waiting for Victor's response. One thing Victor always did was return e-mails promptly. Five minutes passed by. And then another. Nothing. Victor was definitely ignoring me. I thought about calling him, but then remembered he was most likely in the middle of a dressage session at his Malibu ranch where he kept his horses. It was odd that Victor would be off playing with his horses and incommunicado in the middle of a major stock crisis. On second thought, perhaps this was a blessing in disguise because the thought of hearing his sinister, calculating drawl was revolting. The last thing I wanted to hear was another one of his intimidating threats or sexual come-ons. *Pig!*

By four thirty, the late afternoon sun cast a shadow in my office. I was bleary-eyed. Jet lag was setting in, and I was emotionally drained from the events of the day. Via intercom, I let Vivien know that I would be leaving early.

"Only a half-day today, Gloria?" The thick sarcasm in her voice made my skin crawl. There was only one upside to losing my job—never having to see her or her scumbag father again.

"I'll be working from home." The calm tone of my voice hid my fury.

"Then there's no need for me to stay. See you tomorrow, Gloria."

I simply ended the conversation. I was too weary to argue with her. And truthfully, if I didn't have to see her brazen face one more time today, all the better.

As I packed my briefcase with paperwork I needed to catch up on, my cell phone rang. I pressed answer.

"Gloria..."

My heart leapt into my throat. Jaime!

"I'm busy."

"Bullshit."

Damn him!

"Hang up the phone and activate your Skype."

"No."

"Do it." A stern command. "I need to see if we can work this way together."

I submitted. Damn it! I submitted. The effect this powerful sex god could have on me was nothing to be proud of.

I clicked onto Skype, and my eyes almost jumped out of their sockets. Facing me on my large computer screen was Jaime Zander, kneeling on his duvet-covered bed in his hotel suite. His sculpted torso was bare, and a pair of white sweats hung dangerously low on his hips. A sizeable tent bulged between his legs. The air escaped my lungs. I was speechless.

A bemused smile flickered on his drop-dead gorgeous face. "Gloria, you look stressed."

That was the understatement of all times. "I think we should end this."

"Be my guest. You just have to click onto the little red terminate button."

My heart palpitating, I stared at my computer screen. The terminate icon was one touch away. I raised my trembling hand, moved my middle finger to my mouse, and then froze. The sparkling *toi et moi* ring beamed in my face. I couldn't do it.

This was insane. There was so much on my mind. Victor's threat. The fate of the company. My pending doom. But all I could focus on was Jaime Zander's ripped body on my computer screen. I couldn't take my eyes off his chiseled pecs, washboard abs, and that perfect pelvic V. I ran my fingers over his body and could virtually feel every honed muscled...and the rigid length between his thighs.

He shot me a cocky, triumphant smile. "Have you ever role played, Gloria?"

"No." Warmth bloomed between my legs. Now where was his creativity taking us?

He smiled sheepishly. "By the way, Gloria, you look stunning on my iPad. Is that a red Chanel suit you're wearing?"

"Yes," I murmured.

"So powerful. I assume the lace underwear beneath your suit is red too. Red becomes you."

"Yes...and thank you." My voice was small.

"Gloria, listen to me carefully. I want you to lock your door and then take off your suit—the jacket, the blouse, the skirt. When you're done, I want you to crawl onto your desk."

I stunned myself and did as he asked. After shedding my clothes, I scrambled onto my desk and sat back on my heels.

He scanned my body. "You're so fucking hot, Gloria. If I were there, I would bite off all those sweet bows on that sexy underwear of yours and pull down those red-hot panties."

My heated body quivered at his words. "Do you want me to take them off?"

His eyes lowered. I could tell he was gazing at my pussy, pondering how wet it already was. The truth...I was drenched.

"No. That little bow in the center is too cute. It's like your pussy is in a gift-wrapped package."

Tingles zapped the area as another rush of moisture settled between my thighs. My already rapid heartbeat accelerated. My breathing grew shallow.

"Gloria, massage those glorious breasts of yours."

Trance-like, I cupped my bountiful mounds in my hands and squeezed them, languidly circling them together and apart. My thumbs rolled around my sensitive nipples. They hardened beneath the delicate lace of my underwire bra as awareness of my aroused core filled me. I could feel another layer of wetness permeating the crotch of my panties. I closed my eyes as the tingling in my core radiated through me. I was beginning to think I could make myself come just from stimulating my breasts.

"Open your eyes, Gloria, and look at your computer screen."

My eyes almost popped out of their sockets one more time. Jaime was now stark naked, and his huge, erect cock was pointed at me. I was having a heart attack, but not the 911 kind that sent you to the hospital. Although that could very well happen.

He curled his long fingers around his enormous erection, sliding his grip up and down the thick shaft. His hips undulated with the movement of his hand.

"Gloria, I'm on fire." A rapturous expression washed over his gorgeous face. His eyes were smoldering, and his lush mouth parted as he arched his head back and thrust his hips forward.

Flames of desire licked at my core. I, too, was on fire. I let out a moan as my hands continued to massage my heavy breasts.

"Put out my fire, Gloria," he moaned back.

"How?"

"You're a firefighter, Gloria. Extinguish the fire with that wet mouth of yours."

I automatically opened my mouth wide. Leaning into the computer screen, I started bopping my head up and down in tandem with his hand movements. Oh my God! His blazing cock was filling my mouth! I could taste it, feel it inside, the hot thickness expanding into the hallows of my cheeks.

"Faster, angel, before I burn up."

I picked up speed, panting with every cyber intake of his incendiary cock. I massaged my breasts harder, sending sparks to my core. A sizzling fire of my own was raging inside me; it was out of control, the flames consuming every fiber of my being. I lowered one hand to the epicenter, my fingertips burning as they stroked the fiery folds. I didn't know how much longer I could hold on before imploding.

"Oh, Gloria!"

I didn't take my eyes off him as his cock jerked, spurting cum all over his beautiful hand. My mouth remained wide open.

"Did you feel me?"

"Yes!" I gasped. I *could* actually feel him come in my mouth, the spasms of his cock vibrating against my tongue and palate. The hot sensation of his release filled my mouth. I gulped.

"Can you taste me?"

"Yes!" It was true! The sweet salty taste invaded my taste buds.

"Now, Gloria!"

As he shouted my name, I squeezed my eyes shut and combusted with a pinch of my clit. Hot embers shot through my body. Oh. My. God.

"Angel, you deserve a medal for that."

His sultry voice brought awareness back into me. Blinking my eyes open, it took me a few seconds to remember where I was. I took in my surroundings. Fuck. I was in my office, sitting half-naked on my desk and shaking from having oral cyber sex with a man I didn't trust. The riot of emotions I felt made my heart race. I glanced at my computer screen. Jaime Zander, now back in his sweats, bare-chested and barefooted, was sitting cross-legged on his bed. There was still a tent, though smaller, between his thighs. That cocky smile of his played on his face and his blue eyes twinkled.

"I think Skyping will be a very effective form of

long distance communication." He blew me a kiss.

The tangle of emotions I was feeling dissolved into rage. He just wanted to prove once again that he could make me fall apart. Control me. I climbed off my desk and scrambled to put my suit back on.

"Gloria, where are you going?"

"I'm going home," I snapped back at him as I zipped up my skirt. I quickly donned my silk blouse and jacket, not bothering to button it. Damn him! The rogue had rendered me powerless. I just didn't need this in my life when the future of Gloria's Secret and its leader was at stake. I needed, more than ever, to be in control. What was wrong with me?

"Why don't you stop by Shutters before you go home." His voice was seductive.

His words dug a hole in the pit of my stomach. *To warm him up before his hot date?* "I have a previous commitment." I coldly repeated his own earlier words.

He raised his brows. "Oh, with a friend?"

My thumb unconsciously twisted his ring. "A man. So, if you'll excuse me, I have to go. Enjoy your dinner."

"Gloria—"

I ended the Skype session. I hastily grabbed my purse and my briefcase and dashed out of my office.

To my relief, Vivien wasn't at her desk; she was long gone. An unsettling dark thought flashed into my head. The possibility existed that she might be working with Jaime Zander while I was out on the streets on my ass. Jobless and heartsick. I shuddered.

∞

I was happy to be back in my apartment. As soon as I unlocked the door, I tossed my purse and briefcase onto the entryway console and wound up the marble stairs to my bedroom. Plopping down on my bed, I wearily shed my suit and undergarments, glad to be free of my soaking wet bikini panties. The throbbing between my legs had died down, but I couldn't get the image of Jaime Zander, naked on his bed, out of my mind, or forget the feeling of his cock exploding in my mouth.

Today's events whooshed around in my head like a roller coaster—the plane ride, Victor's assault, the stock crisis, Vivien's audacious behavior, Jaime's cyber sex. They were all too much for one human being. I truthfully couldn't think straight. My mind was mush.

Draping a thick fluffy Egyptian cotton robe on my battered body, I ambled to the state-of-the-art bathroom that was adjacent to my bedroom. Perhaps a shower would wash away the mess in my head and bring me some clarity.

Shrugging off the robe, I stepped into my large stall shower, pulled out the faucet knobs, and let the multiple jets of water bombard me. Wasted, I sagged down the travertine wall and buried my head between my bent knees, wishing the memories away. It was futile. My life was spinning out of control, and there was nothing I could do to stop it. Slowly, I lifted my heavy head, my eyes passing over my shiny white scar. As if I didn't have enough going on in my head, the memory of that fateful night flickered inside it. Regardless of how evil Boris

Borofsky was, I had committed a crime. Robbed him blind. I was not a religious person, but I believed in karma. Clarity hit me like a thunderstorm's first sting of rain. There was no doubt. All the terrible things that were happening to me were the result of my terrible secret. There was a power higher than Victor Holden, and He was bringing me down.

I was already in comfy sweats when my cell phone rang. Revitalized a little from the shower, I sprinted downstairs to my purse to answer it. My heart skittered. I hoped it wasn't Jaime. Or Victor. Reaching into my monstrous bag, I sighed with relief when I saw on the caller ID screen that it was Kevin. I pressed answer.

"Glorious, I have to cancel the pity party. All hell is breaking loose. The Associated Press picked up on the *Times* story, and it's going to be everywhere."

"Fuck." *Fuck. Fuck. Fuck.*

"I'm going to be glued to my phone and computer all night dealing with this."

"Kev, did you know that Victor was the first to sell off a shitload of shares?"

Kevin was as surprised as I was and was even more surprised that the press hadn't jumped on it. He agreed with me that we should keep it our little secret until I knew more; right now, the less the press knew, the better.

Kevin heaved a sigh. "I've got to go. I've got three calls coming in."

"I'm so sorry, Kev. No worries about tonight. And besides, I'm zonked and should go to sleep early.

Tomorrow's going to be a living nightmare."

"Do you want me to stay with you tonight? I can work from your place."

"No, I'll be okay." Oh, my Kev! Always there for me.

"Well, if you change your mind, you know where to find me."

A faint smile played on my face. "I'll call you if I need you. Good luck with everything, and let me know of anything major."

After exchanging good-byes, I took my cell phone with me and wandered over to my kitchen. I yanked opened the refrigerator door. Having been away for over a week, it was almost bare. Tilda, my beloved housekeeper, had done a thorough sweep of all my leftover business meals and minimal groceries. There wasn't even any milk for my morning coffee. All that remained was a half-drunk bottle of wine from my last pity party with Kevin and a small chunk of brie cheese. I bit into the cheese and washed it down with a gulp of wine, straight from the bottle. I polished off the rest of it and then headed back upstairs.

I was wiped out. Usually, I had a nighttime beauty routine that consisted of washing my face and slathering my body with Gloria's Secret moisturizer. Not tonight. Not even bothering to take off my sweats, I sunk into my delicious bed and snuggled under the thick duvet. I placed my cell phone, a quick arm's reach away from me on the night table, and then turned off the light. The twinkling lights of the city flickered on the walls. I didn't use blackout shades or blinds because I was afraid to sleep in total darkness by myself.

But tonight, I was also afraid to go to sleep because I dreaded waking up in the morning. I was going to have to deal with all the negative press and the wondering looks of my beloved employees. And then there would be a bombardment of e-mails coming in from store managers and vendors from around the world, inquiring about the future of the company and my own.

Sleep finally claimed me, but not for long. I descended into another kind of darkness.

The song "Gloria" is blasting. Sky-high flames engulf a long runway. Familiar faces flicker in the flames. Once supermodel angels, they're now monsters, their red lipstick-smeared faces distorted and deformed, horns sprouting from their heads. Like a Greek chorus, they chant Gloria over and over.

"Take your final bow, Gloria." The voice is sinister. I recognize it. Victor!

Naked, I hesitantly step onto the runway. The flames surround me, licking at my flesh.

An apparition appears before me. Vivien! She's clad in a black leather corset, fishnet stockings, mile high black boots, and wielding a whip. "Soon, they'll be singing my name!" She snaps her whip at me and cackles.

I cry out in pain. My flesh burns. I run away from her before she strikes again.

In the distance, ahead of me, a God rises from the flames. Jaime! The flames lick at his bare sculpted body, but he's immune to their lethal flicks.

"Gloria, come for me," he calls out, his voice a deep rasp.

I want to run into his arms. Run to safety!

I pick up my pace, propelling my legs to run as fast as they can. My limbs are burning and so are my lungs. No matter how far or fast I run, I cannot reach Jaime.

"Suffer, Gloria!" another voice from behind me calls out.

I steal a glance over my shoulder. Another hideous monster! Crimson blood pours out from two apertures bracketing his snarling mouth. His eyes glow pink.

"Nobody steals from Boris Borofsky!"

He's after me. Oh, God, why can't I run faster?

My punishment: just like the lyrics of the song, I'm always on the run now.

Running away from Victor. From Vivien. From Boris.

Running after Jaime. But no matter how much I run, I never get closer to him. The runway from hell never ends.

Oh the pain! My legs, my lungs, they hurt so much!

But not as much as my heart, that aches for the man of my dreams. "Oh, Jaime!"

"Gloria!" he calls out to me, his arms open wide.

The choir: "Gloria, Gloria, Gloria, Gloria..."

Writhing, I snapped my eyes open and clapped my hands to my ears. The voices in my head wouldn't stop. "Stop it!" I screamed. At last, they faded. My breathing was harsh, and I was bathed in cold sweat. Fear sent shudders rippling through me. My dream...it was symbolically telling me something. I had to face the reality that the world was coming down upon me. Hell awaited me.

Chapter 7

M Y NIGHTMARE HAD JUST GIVEN way to sleep when my cell phone rang. My eyes glued shut, I flung my arm out from under the duvet and fumbled for it on the nightstand. I put it to my ear. My eyes flew open. Kevin! I glanced at my alarm clock; it was just a little after 6:00 a.m. Kevin calling me at this still dark hour signaled bad news. My brain snapped awake, and I bolted to an upright position.

"Glorious, all hell has broken loose. The stock market opened, and there was another big sell-off. Shares have dropped another ten points...and it could get worse as the day goes on."

"God fucking damm it!" The word "fuck" was going to be on the tip of my tongue all day long.

"*The Wall Street Journal* wants to do an interview with you later this morning."

"Tell them NO!" My voice was harsh.

"What about *Forbes? Business Week?* Or the *Financial Times?*"

"Tell them all NO!" I shouted each word.

There was a moment of silence on Kevin's end before he said, "Glorious, you're going to have to issue a statement."

My eyes narrowed with rage. "Simply tell them that Gloria Long assures all her stockholders that

Gloria's Secret is poised for growth. She will not be stepping down as CEO any time soon."

Kevin sighed into the phone. "Got it. I'm heading into the office now."

"I'll see you soon." Nausea rose to my chest. "One last thing, Kev...could you please set up a company-wide meeting in the theater at eleven o'clock. Our employees need to hear what's going on from me. And let's be sure it can be streamed live to stores around the world."

"Will do. I love you, Glorious."

"I love you too." I ended the phone call and mentally picked out the black power suit and shoes I was going to wear today. Armor was what I really needed for the battle ahead.

Before showering, I quickly checked my iPhone calendar. My breath hitched. I had one other major meeting in the afternoon. Fuck. How could I forget? Jaime Zander was coming by at two. Not only did I need armor to get through the day; I also needed a chastity belt. Unfortunately, that was the one item you'd never find in a Gloria's Secret catalogue.

The air in the office was thick with tension; a knife couldn't cut through it. Glum-looking employees avoided eye contact with me as I passed through the halls to my office. I held my head high and greeted them with casual hellos as if it were just another normal day at work.

To my surprise, Vivien was already at her desk. She never came in before me. Never. When I asked her once, "What time do you aim for?", Miss Bitchy

and Entitled replied, "You're lucky I even show up."
She had no appreciation for the first-hand executive
training I was giving her. Absolutely none.

Even more surprising, Vivien seemed to be in
a very cheerful mood. A wide toothy smile spread
across her face when I bid her "good morning."

"Can I get you a coffee?" she asked sweetly.

My brows jumped up. That was a first. I always
had to ask her several times to fetch me a coffee,
and when she finally acquiesced, it was always
accompanied by resentful pout. Most of the time, it
was just easier to get the coffee myself.

"Thanks," I replied. "I'd really appreciate that."

She stood up from her desk, and for the first
time, I could see her entire ensemble. Surprise
again. She was dressed for success in a chic little
black suit that was not that dissimilar from mine.
She was wearing sheer black stockings, black suede
pumps, and a red velvet headband that held back
her inky mane.

"I'll be right back." Her feline eyes twinkled.

As she stepped away, I marveled at this all new
and improved Vivien. Had she finally turned a
corner?

I strode into my office and, once seated at my
desk, turned on my computer. My stomach churned.
Just as I'd expected, there was a slew of inquiring
e-mails in my inbox—seven hundred and fifty-three
new messages to be exact. My heart pounded. I
felt anxious and overwhelmed. I took a long deep
breath to steel myself. On the exhale, I shouted,
"Fuck it!" I wasn't going to open or respond to any of
them...except Kevin's confirming the company-wide

meeting in the theater at eleven.

Five minutes later, Vivien was in my office with my coffee. She placed the steaming mug on a coaster on my desk. A quick peek told me she'd prepared it just the way I liked it with a lot cream.

I took a sip. The aromatic brew wafted up my nose as the hot smooth liquid traveled down my throat. I thanked Vivien again and took another sip.

"Gloria, I just want to apologize for my behavior lately."

I almost spit out my coffee. An apology? This was not the Vivien I knew and despised.

She continued, her raspy voice soft and sincere. "I know you've been under a lot of stress, and I should have been more sensitive to it."

"Yes, that's true."

"I know you're super busy today with the stock crisis and all, but I was wondering if you could meet me for a drink at The Ivy right after work. I'd like to have a conversation with you about my future here and bettering our relationship."

I lowered my mug to my desk and mulled over her words. I was perplexed by her sudden change in both attitude and attire. One thing I was sure about was that if I didn't choose to meet with her, Daddy would know about it. I just didn't need more of Victor Holden in my life.

"Please. It would mean a lot to me, Gloria." The corners of her pink gloss-coated lips curled up into a demure smile.

Another thought crossed my mind. Maybe she could tell me why her father had been among the first to sell off a boatload of shares. He still hadn't responded to my e-mail and he wasn't answering my calls.

"Sure," I finally said. "Why don't we say at six thirty?"

Vivien's smile broadened. "That would be perfect." As she pivoted toward the door, she added, "Just let me know if you need anything else, especially for the big meeting at eleven."

I twitched a smile. "Thanks. I will."

As she strutted out the door, my lips returned to my coffee cup. Sipping the tasty brew, I found it a little odd that Vivien had chosen a restaurant bar close to the hotel where Jaime Zander was staying. It was probably just a coincidence. To the best of my knowledge, neither she nor her father knew that Jaime was in town. And the truth was, The Ivy's charming Caribbean-inspired bar was a favorite watering hole for many of our employees, from top executives right on down to ambitious assistants. It was a place to chill and seek hook-ups. I let it go, and focused on what I was going to tell my anxious employees at the eleven o'clock company-wide meeting.

It took me a half hour at my computer to come up with the words I wanted to share. After a lot of cuts, pastes, and deletes, my speech ended up being short and to the point. I just needed to communicate to my hard-working employees that they had nothing to worry about. No one was getting fired and I was going nowhere. As I read it over, memorizing the words, Kevin, clad in black leather jeans and a tight tee, came running into my office. Holding a large Gloria's Secret pink shopping bag in his hand, he was breathless and wide-eyed. "Glorious, you've got to see this!"

Panic gripped me. There must be a shitload of newspapers inside the bag reporting on the stock crisis and my demise.

Kevin dug inside the bag and my eyes widened. He proudly held up our newest addition to the Gloria's Secret product line—the prototype vibrator for the line of sex toys we were launching in the summer.

"Oh my God, Kev, let me see it."

He handed me the vibrator. Curved slightly like a banana, it featured a sleek shiny white base with control buttons that give way to six inches of sparkly hot pink stimulation. Holding it in my right hand, I curled my left hand fingers around it and ran them up to the rounded tip. Easy to hold. Smooth to the touch. Not too hard, not too soft. Cock-like. Whimsical yet seductive to the eye. Based on extensive research, I'd never seen one like it.

"Don't you love it, Glorious?" gushed Kevin. He was literally doing a "happy dance," shuffling from one foot to the other.

"It's fabulous. I think women are going to love it. Men, too!"

"Totally agree. I'm going to send out a press release this morning."

"No, don't."

Kevin's grin morphed into a frown. "Why not?"

"It's not a good time with the stock crisis. Plus, we need to focus group test it first. Make sure we're giving women what they want."

Kevin nodded. "You're right. There are two dozen more. I'll make sure Consumer Insights sets up the groups." He laughed. "I don't think we'll have any problem getting respondents."

For the first time in god knows how many hours, I laughed too. It felt good to dispel all the doom and gloom—even for a short minute.

"Do you want to hold on to the vibrator?" Kevin asked before heading to the door.

"Yes."

He set it upright on my desk and sashayed off. My eyes stayed fixed on the slick erect fixture, our stunning new sex toy. There was only one way this company and I were going—and that was up. Suddenly, a brilliant idea hit me. I e-mailed Kevin. Already back in his office a few doors down from mine, he immediately e-mailed me back: *G—That's genius! I'll make it happen. xoK*

At 11 a.m., I was standing on the stage of our packed state-of-the art theater, a former screening room, where we often held large sales presentations, product announcements, and pep rallies. Every seat was taken. My eyes swept across the audience of employees, taking in the anxious expressions on their faces. It made me proud how much diversity there was among them—all races were represented as were ages. Our company policy was not to discriminate against anyone, regardless of age or socio-economic background. We were a proud equal opportunity employer.

Behind me, the large screen we often used for sales presentations and commercial screenings was pulled down.

I began by thanking everyone for coming. My welcome was followed by a loud applause. And then

I steeled myself.

"By now, you all know that that we have been experiencing a stock crisis. I am here to tell you that it is unfounded. Our company is as robust as ever—thanks to all of you and your fellow employees around the world."

Applause.

I cleared my throat and continued. "Many of you have IRA's and shares of Gloria's Secret stock. Do not worry. I promise you that the price of the stock will soar even higher than it was before. You will all have money for your children's education and your retirements."

More applause, even louder.

Tears pricked my eyes. I took in a deep breath. "And I'm here to tell you that I'm going nowhere. No one can bully me and force me to leave the company I built with my own blood, sweat, and tears."

To my astonishment, employees rose to their feet in a standing ovation. Throughout the theater, they were cheering, "Go, Gloria!"

It took all I had to battle tears. I was so overwhelmed by their enthusiastic response. I had always been there for my employees, and now they were there for me. My eyes circled around the theater, landing on the faces of so many who I personally knew—from sales execs and seamstresses to tech gurus and janitors. In the front row, Kevin was applauding wildly, but standing listlessly next to him was Vivien. In contrast to her earlier cheerleader behavior, she now seemed to be feigning enthusiasm, if any. Her fingertips lethargically tapped together and, I swear, she was rolling her eyes. When she caught my eyes on her, she pasted a big plastic smile on her face and applauded with zeal. *Strange.*

I moved on to the final leg of my speech, trying to quiet the audience with downward waves of my hands. "I'm going to end this little speech on an up note." An image of the vibrator flashed onto the large screen behind me.

"Introducing Gloria's Secret latest breakthrough—My Secret Vibrator. We're going to blow the competition out of the water. There's only one way we're going—and that's up with a bang!"

The audience went wild. Shrieks and gasps accompanied the loud applause.

A big smile broke out across my face. "Thank you all. Now get back to work!"

I ran down the steps to the stage and darted out the side door of the theater. I could still hear clapping and cheering. Kevin met me in the hallway and gave me a big bear hug.

"That was fan-fucking-tastic, Glorious!"

"Thanks, Kev," I said humbly. I was emotionally and physically drained.

We walked back together to our respective offices. After dropping him at his, I continued on two more doors to mine. Vivien had beaten me back. She was filing her nails but quickly tucked the emery board under her desk mat when she set her eyes on me.

That big fake smile flashed on her face. "Oh, Gloria, you were amazing. I want to give a speech like that when I'm CEO."

Although there was sincerity in her voice, her comment sent a shiver up my spine. I gave myself a mental kick. I was just being over-sensitive, maybe borderline paranoid about the tenacity of my job.

I simply said, "Thanks. Any important new e-mails or phone calls come in?"

Vivien leaned into her computer screen and shook her head. She gazed up at me. "Gloria, by the way, I forgot to tell you. I have to leave early today right after lunch. I have a doctor's appointment. It's all the way out in the Valley so it's unlikely I'll be coming back. I hope you're okay with that." Her eyes stayed locked on mine as she awaited my response.

"Not a problem. I hope everything's all right."

A sweet smile accompanied a flutter of her fake lashes. "Oh, yes, everything's just fine."

I couldn't help furrowing my brows. She was probably going to one of her "beauty" doctors —for dermabrasion, Botox, or lip filler. Now that I knew she was older than the twenty-nine years she claimed to be, perhaps she had a genuine need for these treatments. I forced myself not to say another word. She was being supportive, and I needed Daddy's little girl on my side. Besides, at two o'clock, Jaime Zander was scheduled to meet with me. In light of their tumultuous, borderline incestuous past and her recent come-ons, I was glad she wouldn't be here.

Once inside my office, I bounded to my desk and immediately started responding to the e-mails I'd received directly. Already several hundred more were sitting in my inbox pursuant to my speech. One by one, I painstakingly went though them. Virtually all of them were supportive, bringing much needed joy to my heart. I typed away feverishly, intermittently checking the price of Gloria's Secret stock. Damn it!

It had tumbled another five points. Maybe my speech had cheered up employees, but it did nothing to shake off investor anxiety. I took a break from the e-mails and slumped down in my chair. I was in no mood to meet with Jaime Zander—nor did I have the time. I had no choice; though it was already 1:45, I needed to cancel our meeting. I whipped out my cell phone and texted him.

> ME: *Must cancel meeting*
> JZ: *Don't. That's rude.*
> ME: *I have a crisis.*
> JZ: *I know. Hang in there.*
> ME: *It's intense.*
> JZ: *You'll get thru it.*
> ME: *You have no clue.*
> JZ: *I do. Trust me.*

Again, those unnerving two words "trust me." I steeled myself as I responded.

> ME: *PLZ don't come.*
> JZ: *Too late.*
> ME: *Huh?*
> JZ: *I'm here*

Shit! My intercom buzzed. Sure enough, it was Claudia announcing Jaime Zander's arrival. My heart raced at the mention of his name. I mentally kicked myself for letting him have this effect on me, but there was nothing I could do about it. I told Claudia that I would meet him in reception myself. Composing myself, I rose from my desk and, in slow motion, trod over to the large ornate standing mirror in the corner of my office. I studied myself. My reflection frightened me. I looked dissipated. My complexion was wan, and dark shadows circled my two-toned eyes. I adjusted my chaste suit and quickly re-braided my hair, letting it fall around my shoulder. I had to confess: I wanted to look my best for Jaime Zander. Before heading out the door, I reapplied some red lipstick. I frowned. No matter how hard I tried, Gloria Long, the powerful leader, looked more like a wounded soldier.

When I dragged myself to reception, I found Jaime seated on one of the white leather couches, making small talk with Claudia. He was wearing loose, low-waisted drawstring pants that exposed his toned thighs beneath the lightweight linen fabric, and a white V-neck tee that flaunted his tanned biceps and taut chest. On his feet were casual red topsiders that he wore sockless. His collar-length, windblown hair was parted in the middle, and he had shaved. But there was still fine layer of stubble outlining his strong, dimpled jaw and circling his kissable lips. My heart fluttered. Mr. Sexy Laidback looked swoonworthy, something that was not lost on Claudia. Or on me. I so wanted to run my hand over his face and then through his tousled hair. Bantering with him, goo-goo eyed Claudia twirled her flaming red curls around her fingers. Her flirtatious behavior elicited a small pang of jealousy that made me uncomfortable. Confession: I'd never been jealous of other women until I met this magnetic man.

"Hello, Mr. Zander." I forced my voice to sound very businesslike.

Jaime's denim blues twinkled when he saw me. He jumped up from the couch and met me halfway. I had the burning urge to fall into his taut, sculpted chest, but refrained. He tipped up my chin. From the corner of my eye, I could see Claudia gawk.

"You look stressed, Ms. Long."

"I am. I'm under a lot of pressure."

"I know. The stock sell off has been all over the Internet and news."

"I don't know how to stop it."

A tear leaked out of one eye. Jaime gently brushed it away. The mere touch of him was making me weak with desire.

"I hope you understand I don't have a lot of time right now or energy. I can give you a quick tour." I immediately regretted my offer, as the size of the Gloria's Secret complex with its manufacturing plant and design showroom was daunting.

He affectionately tugged at my braid. "Why don't we start in your office?"

Suddenly, I felt lightheaded. I don't know if was the stress, the scent of him, or the very sight of him. Or his touch. My knees buckled.

"Angel!" he cried out as he caught me and scooped me up in his strong arms. I swear Claudia practically swooned herself when I looped my limp arms around his neck. The edges of his silky hair and brought me back to the moment.

"Thanks," I murmured.

"Gloria, you need to chill. Tell me the way."

I released a sigh and sunk into him. I might

as well enjoy the ride, drained as I was. As I led the gorgeous, sexy as sin god back to my office, I couldn't help noticing every female eye on him. His magnetism was a force to be reckoned with. I knew from first-hand experience. I flushed with embarrassment.

"Do you know that every woman we pass has her eyes on you?"

"Yeah. But I have my eyes on only one. You."

My breath hitched. At the door to my office, he smashed his lips onto mine. I was too worn out to resist. I only wished that Vivien could be here to witness his kiss. On second thought, I was glad she wasn't.

He crossed the threshold of my office, slamming the door behind him and locking it.

Once inside, Jaime sat down with me on his lap on a pink velvet love chair, never losing contact with my lips. Damn it. I was losing myself in him again. I couldn't let this happen. I had too many other fires to quell. With difficulty, I broke away and caught my breath.

"Mr. Zander, this was not an appointment to fuck me."

"Who said I was going to fuck you, Ms. Long?" he responded as his eyes took in my hot pink and white boudoir-like office. They lingered on my desk.

"Is that what I think it is on your desk?"

Though slightly embarrassed, I nodded with pride. "My Secret Vibrator. It's the prototype for our new product line."

"So you're doing a line of sex toys. That's brilliant, Gloria."

Lifting me off his lap onto the petite couch, he

strode over to my desk and then returned with the sex toy in his hand. He loomed in front of me. I was melting under the gaze of this sexy beast.

He studied the vibrator, gliding his other hand up and down it. "It's an erotic work of art."

"Thanks. We put a lot of research into the design. We wanted it to be curvy and seductive with a bit of whim like the rest of our brand." I admired the hot pink vibrator with its sleek white handle and signature pink heart switch.

"Have you tested it yet?"

"We're doing some focus groups later this month."

A diabolical smirk whipped across his face. "Gloria, I meant have *you* tested it?"

A sudden pool of wetness gathered between my thighs, and my insides jolted. I was too taken back by his question to say a word. I nervously shook my head, getting a sense as to where this meeting was going.

His eyes bore into me, heating me further. "I agree that consumer research is very important, but I think you need to test it first so you can better evaluate your focus group results."

I stiffened. "Are you asking me to play with this vibrator?"

"No, Gloria, I'm ordering you. Lift up your skirt."

"I don't have time for this."

"Yes, you do. It's important. And you know it."

With quivering fingers, I did as he asked, scrunching the tight pencil skirt up as far as it would go. To my surprise, it went all the way to my hips.

He flicked the switch on. The buzzing rang in my

ears. "Hold this." He thrust the buzzing toy into my hand, and in one smooth move, yanked down my garter, panties, and stockings to my ankles. Pulling off my heels, he tore all the garments off me and tossed them to the floor. "Now, bend your knees and spread your legs."

I did as I was told. My heart was hammering.

"Perfect, Gloria. I have a beautiful view of that glorious pussy of yours."

My core muscles twitched and my breathing hitched.

"Now, we're going to do some one-on-one research. It's just like a focus group... only more intimate. Just you and me. I'm going to ask you some questions, and you'll do your best to respond to them honestly. Are you ready?"

"Yes," I said breathlessly. I hadn't even put the toy to my glistening folds, and my nerve endings were already sparking with tingles.

"Good. Now put the vibrator to your pussy and just experiment with it."

Hesitantly, I put the vibrator to my sex. I gasped. It was like nothing I'd ever felt before— the buzzing sensation so different from Jaime's nimble fingers. I bravely ran the head up and down my slick folds and then lingered on my clit, circling the warm tip around the hypersensitive button. A gasp escaped my throat as my stimulated clit lit up. It felt amazing!

"Do you like the way it feels, Gloria?"

"Yes!"

"Can you describe the sensations?"

Oh, God. How could I put what I was feeling into words? It reminded me a little of being on the back of Kevin's second-hand Honda scooter, our means of transportation when we first came to LA. "They're like relentless buzzing tickles," I spluttered as the toy zapped my clit, making it pulse with pleasure. "The kind that you crave and can't stand at the same time."

He fired another question at me. "How does it make you feel?"

This time, my loud moans were my answer. The tremors intensified to the point of unbearable. My pulse raced. Was this beautiful torture or tortuous pleasure? *Semantics.* I couldn't sit still. Writhing, I squeezed my eyes shut. *BUZZZZZ!* Oh my God. As the insane, intense pressure built, I didn't know what I'd do first—faint or come.

"Gloria, be more specific. Does it make you want to fall apart?"

"Yes!" I panted. I didn't know much longer I could hold on before passing out.

"Are you on the verge of an orgasm?"

"YES!"

"What does it feel like?"

Duh! "Like I'm going to come!" All hell broke loose between my legs. I shrieked with relief as my desperate release took hold of me. The flutters between my legs spiraled upward like a buzzing swarm of bees. I had buzzed my way to pure, utter ecstasy.

"How do you feel now, Gloria?"

"Fuck!" I muttered as the buzzing inside me persevered. No other words sprung to my parched mouth. I fluttered my eyes open. Still looming above me, Jaime Zander eyed me rapturously. He had taken off his linen drawstring pants. Between his mighty thighs, his divine cock jutted in its full erect glory. I salivated at the sight of it. My throbbing sex was wet with want.

A cocky grin flickered on his gorgeous face. "We're not done with our little research session, Gloria. I want to know—did using the vibrator increase your libido?"

"Yes," I said, my voice a raspy whisper. I was desperate for him, drenched with desire and despair.

"Do you want me to fuck you, Gloria?"

"Yes!" I begged. "Please!"

A satisfied smile spread across his face. His lustful eyes circled around my office. "Where would you like to be fucked—over your desk or we could do it right here?"

"Here!" I mouthed. I couldn't wait. I so bloody needed him inside me.

"Perfect." In one swift smooth move, he yanked up my legs and leveraged the heels of my feet on his shoulders. He leaned into me, anchoring one hand on the back of the love chair for support and using the other to drive his rock-hard cock into my ready entrance. Because I was so wet, he penetrated me quickly and easily. My back arched at the fullness of his exquisite invasion. I let out a moan.

"Oh, Gloria, you feel so fucking good," he groaned as he began to grind his cock inside me. I was awed by how deep he could go in this position. I shrieked with pleasure each time he hit my G-for-Gloria spot and thrust my hips to meet his touch. Raw, guttural grunts accompanied his truculent plundering. The sounds of our moaning and groaning, combined with our pounding hearts and ragged pants, drowned out the sound of the humming vibrator. I almost forgot about it until I felt Jaime slide it out of my hand.

I met his gaze. His beautiful face was glazed with sweat. I brushed away the damp strands of hair that'd fallen forward into his hooded blue eyes. He breathed into me. "We're now going to find out if this little toy of yours makes sex more pleasurable for the women *and* her partner."

How much better could it get? His relentless deep strokes were taking the air out of my lungs—and his—and blowing my brain apart.

"We're also going to take it up a couple of notches." I heard two clicks of the vibrator control. Fuck. I'd forgotten this contraption had three levels of stimulation— mild, moderate, and intense. Our research had shown that not all women are the same. I'd had it set on the first level and that was almost unbearable. Jaime had adjusted it to the extreme.

Insane pressure was building readily inside me, my climax just a heartbeat away. When the loud, amped up vibrator, once again touched down on my clit, I could no longer hold back. My slick bundle of nerves gave way as wave after fierce wave of ecstasy like I'd never known before ripped through me. My whole body shook.

He breathed into my ear as my orgasm consumed me. "So answer the question. It's important. Does this vibrator make the sex better?"

"Oh, YES!" *Yes, yes, yes!*

"I'd have to agree."

With a growl of approval, he thrust hard into me again, and as I came one more time, I screamed out his name.

"Gloria!" I heard him roar almost at once as his own climax met mine in shuddering victory. Someone, for sure, was going to call security.

"Oh, angel," he moaned, this time softly as he rode his orgasm out. "That was fucking amazing."

A long, melodic sigh was all I could manage. He had taken my breath away. I was still quivering all over, and beads of sweat claimed every inch of my body.

Slowly, he pulled out of me and lowered my feet to the couch. They were tingly numb like the rest of me. I didn't think I'd ever be able to get up from the couch or walk again.

My eyes stayed locked on him as he pulled his white linen pants up over his still pumped up cock. After tying them, he flopped down on the couch, sliding me back into his lap. Still trembling, I curled up my knees and snuggled against him, the softness of his tee a delicious contrast to his rock hard chest. He coiled my braid around his hand and kissed the top of my head.

"So, Gloria," he breathed into my ear, "I think our *in depth* research suggests that your toy has tremendous potential. You should definitely consider expanding the product line. Maybe hot pink nipple clamps or sparkly love beads. Pretty in pink handcuffs too. The possibilities are endless."

My mind raced. I could picture them all. He was a fucking genius, no pun intended. I sighed into Mr. Creativity, and let him play with my hair.

He nibbled my neck. "And, Gloria, I want to be the one to test them."

"On who?" I asked playfully, damn well knowing

the answer.

He gave me a sweet peck on my cheek. "On my favorite respondent."

He made me smile. He made me let go. And he made me feel alive in a way I'd never known before. While he continued with the hair play and nibbles, I just let myself enjoy the warmth of his manly body. Lost in him, all my troubles melted away. Nirvana.

My state of mindless bliss came to an abrupt halt when my office phone rang. I jolted. With Vivien out of the office, I had to pick it up myself.

"Let it ring," purred Jaime as he nipped at my earlobe.

"I can't. It's probably important." As much as I never wanted to leave his lap, I forced myself up, pulling down my skirt, and somehow made it over to my desk. I don't know how my legs carried me there; they were pure jelly. The throbbing, soreness, and wetness between my inner thighs didn't help at all.

Standing, I picked up the phone. The voice on the other end sent a sharp shiver up my spine. Victor!

His tone was curt. "Gloria, the potential business partner I met with in Paris is here in LA. I've set up lunch for tomorrow—noon at the Polo Lounge. I want you there."

"Fine."

"We need to carry business on as usual."

"Yes, I agree." My voice quivered. I stole a glance at Jaime. His mouth was pressed into a thin angry line; his eyes narrowed, and his fists clenched. He knew who was on the line.

"Don't be late, Gloria," growled Victor.

"I never am."

"Oh, and by the way, have you reconsidered my offer?"

"There's nothing to reconsider, Victor."

"You're going to be sorry, Gloria." He hung up on me before I could ask him why he'd sold off so many shares of stock.

My hand shook as I put the phone down. Reality hit me with the force of a rockslide. Maybe the pep talk I gave to my employees placated their worries and boosted morale, but it didn't make a dent in the mountain of problems I faced. Everything was at stake—my future, my company, and yes, even my heart. Overwhelmed with emotion, I slumped into my desk chair and, uncontrollably, sobbed big ugly tears.

"Sheesh, Angel," shouted Jaime as he sprinted my way. He swept me up into his strong arms and held me tight like a baby. Folding my arms around his neck, I heaved against his broad, taut chest.

"I'm sorry. I'm a fucked up mess," I said hoarsely through my tears. I swiped at them, but they hopelessly kept pouring.

"Angel, let me help." He leaned into me and licked them away.

I gazed up into his long-lashed eyes. "I'm scared. Everything I've ever worked for is going up in smoke. Tomorrow, I may not even have a job."

Jaime's face grew fierce. "Don't let that bastard threaten you. I'm not going let him take you down."

Before I could utter a word, his soft lips latched onto mine and smothered my sobs. My tears seared his face as his kiss deepened, melting not only my mouth but all of me. How safe and empowered I felt in his arms! I could stay in them the rest of my life.

Finally, forcing myself to pull away, I caught my breath. My tears had subsided, but Jaime's face was now as soaked as mine. I lightly ran my hand over his dampened stubble, touching it as if it were fine raw silk. "I should give you that tour now of the company," I managed. Tears rose to my eyes again.

Jaime caught them with his tongue before they could travel down my cheeks. "Angel, we'll do that some other time. Right now, you need to get of here and clear your head."

"I can't leave my office," I protested on the verge of another tsunami.

He gently set me down on my feet. "Yes, you can." He gave me the once-over. I was a pantiless, blubbering, barefoot mess.

"Do you have anything besides your suit to wear? Something more casual?"

"Why?" I asked, straightening my skirt.

"You need to chill, Gloria. Stressing is not going to solve anything. You're headed for a breakdown."

I digested his words. He was right as always. My office had a walk-in closet where I kept emergency business suits and cocktail dresses, spare lingerie, and my yoga clothes. The Gloria's Secret complex even had a gym where employees could work out and where I had my every other day private yoga instruction. Yoga kept me centered and helped me deal with the stress of running a Fortune 500 company. Madame Paulette had preached that "*Feet* bodies make *feet* minds."

"I'll be right back." Padding over to the closet, I could feel his eyes on my backside. I stole a glance backward and shot him a dirty look. He smirked. *Beautiful bastard!*

Two minutes later, I was back in my office, wearing a comfortable pair of Gloria's Secret black yoga pants that hung low on my hips and a matching black tank with a built-in shelf bra that ended on my midriff just above my navel. Our signature pink heart was featured prominently on the seat of the pants as well as on the tank. A pair of simple black flip-flops adorned my feet. Usually, I dressed for success, but now I was dressing to de-stress.

A cocky smile played on Jaime's face at the sight of me. "You look sexy in those."

"Thanks." My clit twitched.

"I bet you look very fuckable when you do a downward facing dog."

The temperature of my already heated body rocketed. Damn him! This Adonis was making me lose control all over again. The ongoing battle between my mind and body was raging.

"I've had second thoughts. I really should get back to work."

"No, Gloria. You can't." He drew me up to him by the drawstring of my stretchy pants. My breasts skimmed his tee shirt, hardening against the friction of his chest, as his fingers trailed down from my navel to my center.

"You're still not wearing panties, are you?" Not waiting for a response, he slipped his hand beneath the waistband and caressed my slick folds. A heat wave was happening right here in my office, and it had nothing to do with global warming.

"Please, Mr. Zander, I really need to get back to

work."

"No!"

"What if Victor stops by?" He did that from time to time, just to intimidate me.

"Fuck, Victor!" Jaime gritted through clenched teeth. "I'm kidnapping you."

In one swift swoop, he threw me over his shoulder.

"Put me down!" I protested, pounding his rippled back.

"You're coming with me. We're going on a ride."

A ride? Holy shit! Was he taking me to the Santa Monica Pier? Was I in store for another Ferris wheel fuck? Or this time was it going to be a roller coaster? Was that his latest creative idea of getting me to fall apart for him?

As he hauled me away, I was once again helplessly and hopelessly his prisoner. Confession: I loved it.

Chapter 8

Fifteen minutes later, Jaime and I were cruising up the coast along the Pacific Coast Highway in the vintage red Thunderbird convertible he had rented. Thank goodness, the Santa Monica Pier was behind us; Jaime Zander had a different destination in mind. The Beach Boys were blasting from the stereo radio, and he was doing his finest impression of Brian Jones. I had to admit he was pretty good. Confession: his pitch perfect voice with just the right amount of throatiness was amazing, and he could even harmonize.

"How come you didn't blindfold me?" I asked, interrupting his *America's Got Talent* sing-along rendition of "Good Vibrations," a fitting song given our most recent sexual encounter.

Without taking his eye off the road, he replied, "Angel, been there; done that. And besides, I wanted you to enjoy the view."

I was grateful for the opportunity. To the left, my eyes took in the sweeping Pacific Ocean with its shimmering turquoise water and white-crested waves. It never ceased to awe me. I loved the ocean and always had. It was magic.

My eyes also took in Jaime. He was wearing black Ray-Bans that sat on the bridge of his manly straight nose. The wind ruffled his silky chestnut hair, and I had to refrain from running my fingers through it. God, he was one sexy beast!

"Where are we going?" I had to shout to make myself heard above the wind and blasting music.

"Some place special." He rested his right hand on my thigh and continued to expertly maneuver the sports car with the other. My braid flapped in the wind, strands breaking loose. Inhaling the fresh salty sea air, I felt all my tension release and just let myself enjoy the beautiful ride. And the beautiful sight of Jaime Zander beside me. I couldn't resist meeting his hand with mine; my fingers clasped his. A smile flickered on his breathtaking face.

About forty minutes into the ride, the Malibu coast, with its clusters of million dollar beach houses, grew more rugged. Waves crashed against jutting rocks, and soon tall trees obscured the view of the sea. Nearing Ventura, Jaime made a sharp left turn into an almost hidden road that led to the ocean. Cypress trees and wild flowers dotted the rocky, serpentine path. Jaime put both hands on the wheel as he expertly navigated it. The bumps along the way sent jolts to my still vibrating core. The road came to a sudden end and he parked the car. I could hear the roar of the ocean below us. The scent of the sea mingled with the sweet smell of jasmine; it was divine enough to bottle. Unbuckling myself, I followed Jaime's lead out of the car before he had a chance to open the passenger door. He came around the car and took my hand. He silently led me down another rustic path laden with multi-color wild flowers and tall grass until we were standing on a cliff above the ocean. The view below of the white-capped waves crashing against the rocky shore was spectacular. I could feel the cool ocean spray against my cheeks. It was just the two of us and the mighty sea; there was no sign of civilization in any direction. This place was magical.

"What is this place?" I asked, breaking our spell of silence.

Jaime gazed at the ocean and a melancholic smile splayed on his face. There was a Zen-like quality to him that I'd never seen before. A whole different side of him exposed. "This is my property."

My eyes widened. "You own all this?"

"Yup...all the way down to the beach. There's five hundred feet of oceanfront land."

I gazed down at the white sandy beach. Seagulls stalked the shoreline in search of food, and dolphins danced in the distance. The ebb and flow of the crashing waves was like music in my ears. We were standing on a piece of heaven on earth.

He continued. "I bought it with the proceeds from the sale of my mother's Bel Air mansion. It's one of the last private enclaves along the coast."

"It's amazing," I said, truly meaning it.

"Thanks. I'm really lucky to own it. My father loved the ocean. When I was little, he used to take me here and paint. Whenever I'm here, I think of him."

My mind flashed back to the paintings in his office. Many of them were seascapes that resembled this spot. The foliage now was more abundant and overgrown. The image of a beautiful, carefree little boy frolicking in this rustic haven as his father painted filled my head and almost brought tears to my eyes.

Jaime kicked at a rock; it flew off the edge, disappearing into the shimmering sand below. He squeezed my hand. "One day, I'm going to build a house here and carve steps into the cliffside that lead down to the ocean."

"You're going to move here from New York?" I glanced down at his *toi et moi* ring. The intertwining heart-shaped diamonds glistened in the sun.

"I want to. Many of my clients are based in California and Asia. It would be more convenient. I'm actually looking for office space while I'm out of here."

The thought of Jaime moving to Los Angeles both unnerved and thrilled me. "Won't you be lonely living all the way out here in a big house all by yourself?"

He remained silent for a long time, staring out to the sea. Then, without warning, he spun me around so that we were face-to-face, just a breath apart. He lifted his sunglasses on top of his head, and his blue gray eyes, the color of the late afternoon sea, gazed deep into mine. My heart hammered as he tipped up my chin.

"I don't plan on living here alone. I'm tired of living in a hotel where people come and go. I'm looking for someone special to share my life with... and I may have found her."

My skin prickled. I said nothing. Words were trapped in my throat.

"Gloria, I've never had a relationship before. I've fucked a lot of women, but none of them has meant a thing to me. They're just mindless, faceless fucks.

You're different, angel. I can never get your face out of my head. When I'm away from you, all I want is to be with you. And when I'm with you, I can't get enough of you. I want to breathe the air you breathe and kiss the ground you walk on. I want to go to sleep with you in my arms and wake up to you on my chest. And I want to fuck you everyway I know how. Make you fall apart and then put you back together again. Over and over. There will never be enough ways to show you how I feel about you. Or words to tell you."

He paused and inhaled deeply. My blood was ringing in my ears as he exhaled and softly said, "Gloria, you make me fall apart too."

This was all too much for me. My emotions were in turmoil, and my mind was in meltdown. I gripped his shoulders before my knees gave out. Tears were forming in my eyes. "Jaime, are you saying you want a real relationship with me?" *You love me?*

He nervously played with my braid. "Yeah, angel, that's what I'm trying to say. I guess it's not my best pitch. I don't do relationships well."

I flashed a little smile. "Neither do I."

He looked straight into my eyes. "Do you want to give it a try?"

My fingers toyed with his *toi et moi* ring. "An official you and me?"

"Yeah...Well?"

My mind was spinning and my heart was thudding. Jesus Christ. Was I ready for a relationship with this beautiful, romantic, sexy god? Could I handle it? The timing couldn't be worse with the stock crisis and my job at stake. It might work. It might not.

And there was still the long distance factor to deal with. Skyping sex did not make for a relationship. Was I just setting myself up to get hurt? He had a fucked a lot of women. And I was just one of them. I mean, he didn't even say he loved me. And hell, I'd only known him for a little over a week though it felt like a lifetime.

Jaime's sultry voice brought my mental ramblings to a halt. He tugged on my braid. "Come on, angel. The suspense is killing me."

If only I could consult Madame Paulette. I pondered—what would she say? Her husky voice sounded in my head. "*Ma chérie*, no *risque* no gain... It *eez* better to have loved and lost than never to have loved at all." Her last words to me whirled around in my head. Come on, who was I fooling? I was madly in love with this man. I wanted him more than he wanted me. I had to take a chance, regardless of the consequences.

"Yes," I finally breathed. "But there's got to be rules. Like—"

Cupping my face, he cut me off. "Gloria, there's only one rule. Don't ever leave me. The rest are meant to be broken." On the loud crash of a wave, his lips crashed onto mine. Every part of me melted into this man as he wrapped me in his arms. Oh, the power of a kiss! The power of this man! Nothing else existed. Our tongues twirled and swirled, dancing in unison to the music of the sea. His hard body pressed into mine, arousing every erotic fiber of my being.

I wanted him. All of him. As he clung to my mouth, I tore at his tee and kept contact, biting right through the fabric as I pulled it over his head. Once it was off, my mouth was greedily back on his.

"Oh, angel," he moaned as I frantically untied his drawstring pants and let them drop to his ankles. There was nothing between them and his flesh. Kicking off his topsiders, he stepped out of the crumpled linen heap. Without delay, I kicked off my flip-flops and yanked off my sweats. His huge erection brushed against my belly.

It wasn't enough. I wanted to feel all of him—every taut muscle, every fine hair, every square inch of his magnificent body. Delirious with lust, I struggled to get my tight tank top over my head.

"Let me help you," he breathed into my ear. In one seamless movement, he lifted the top over my head and pulled me down to the ground. I was sprawled on his naked gorgeousness, my legs straddling him. Face-to-face, we were a tangle of tongues and arms. Our chests rose and fell together. His heavy erection pulsed beneath me.

"I want to make love to you here," I managed on a brief reprieve.

He groaned with pleasure. "Angel, take all of me. You know what to do."

His words sent a wave of wetness to my core, already an erotic sea waiting for him take the plunge. I leveraged myself on the palm of one hand, and with my other, I gripped his thick length and slipped the tip into my opening. His cock dove inside me. My muscles flexed, feverishly drawing him in. He let out a delicious groan. Once he was submerged, his fullness divine, I set my hand down and lowered myself to my elbows so that I was anchored just a little above him. His beautiful face was in mine, our breaths almost one.

"Fuck me!" I cried out.

"No, fuck me!"

I clenched my pussy around him, then lifted myself off his cock and slid back down until the crown hit my womb.

"Oh, Angel!" he groaned with my moan and started pounding away.

Oh, God. Being on top felt so amazing. So empowering. My undulating hips met his every thrust, the penetration as deep as it could get. And as good as it could get with his magnificent cock rubbing against my throbbing clit and hitting my G-spot with each long, hard stroke. His warm hands groped my breasts, squeezing and kneading. I kissed him everywhere I could until my hungry lips latched back onto his mouth, welcoming the invasion of his skillful tongue. Desperate groans escaped my throat. There was no stopping me now.

"Oh, angel, you *do* know what do you," he moaned into my mouth. "You make me feel so fucking good."

"The same," I moaned back as the pressure inside me built to climax. My nails dug into the hard earth; I wanted to hold off, not fall off the cliff, and feel his orgasm before mine. To experience my own power to send him over the edge. That fierce sexual power he had unleashed inside me.

I whimpered as I deepened my own thrusts while his plundering accelerated. In and out. Faster and harder. I knew he was close to coming. Sweat was beading on his forehead with each heavy breath, and his cock was pulsating.

"Oh, Gloria!" he roared as his cock convulsed, spurting its hot seed deep inside me. As he rode out his orgasm, I came hard, shuddering in thunderous waves of ecstasy around him. Gasping for air, I collapsed my head onto his sweat-drenched chest. His contoured pecs brushed against my cheekbones as my ears took in his rapid breaths and heartbeat that drummed with mine. His long fingers threaded through my scalp while I just lay there limp and motionless, my mind and body blown to pieces. I had just made outrageous, passionate love to my man on his heavenly turf. Fucked him where he'd once frolicked and sent him flying over the cliff with me right behind him.

I didn't know how long we'd stayed in that dormant position when Jaime repositioned me so that I was lying on my back right beside him, my head resting on his rock-hard chest, his sculpted arm draped around me. The waves of the ocean bellowed below us, ebbing and flowing in rhythm with my own. All my troubles had washed away with the high tide. All that was in my mind was the beautiful man lying close beside me. Without even gazing at him, I could envision his hooded ocean blue eyes, those lush, kissable lips verging on that contented, cocky smile, and that dimpled chin and perfect nose pointed up at the sky. A peaceful smile splayed across my face.

He broke the long, blissful silence. "So, I guess this is no longer virgin ground."

I laughed against his chest. "Guess not."

He playfully twirled my straggly braid as we watched a billowy cloud roll in.

"My father used to play a game with me here."

My eyes met his gaze. He was still staring at the cloud.

"Use your imagination. What does that cloud look like to you?"

I looked up again and studied the fluffy puff. I was awed. "It looks like a heart. What do you see?"

"I see a woman's body inside a heart."

I gazed at the cloud again. Oh my God. He was right. The way the pink-blue sky intercepted the cloud created that illusion. "I can see it!" I gasped.

Pleased with my vivid imagination, Jaime flicked the tip of my braid across my ticklish neck and plunked a kiss on my cheek. "Did your father ever play games with you?" he asked.

My chest tightened. My lightness of being gave way to darkness.

"I never had a father." My voice was low and monotone.

Jaime shifted. "What do you mean?"

"My mother was a hooker. A crack whore. I was an unwelcome accident. My father could have been anyone she fucked." Tears of shame sprang to my eyes. I had opened up to him. Shared something hidden in my past.

Skimming my breasts, he brushed away my tears. "Gloria, my angel, there's nothing to be ashamed of. If we're going to have a relationship, then we've got to be open and honest with each other. I've shared my scars, and you've got to share yours."

He dusted the tip of my braid across my shimmering scar. "Gloria, did your mother have something to do with this?"

My body stiffened as my heart skipped a beat. How could I tell him the truth behind this scar? So much of me wanted to blurt it out to this man I now belonged to, but I knew the moment I confessed my misdoing, my secret, he would leave me in a heartbeat. I tried hard to banish the memory. As always, it was futile. That nightmarish night replayed in my head in its full gory horror. A cool ocean breeze sent a shiver all over me and brought me back to the moment.

"No, she didn't," I stammered. "I ran away from her." At least, I was being truthful about my relationship with her.

"Is she still alive?"

"I don't know. And I don't care. I'm sure she feels the same way."

His eyes stayed fixed on the scar, his expression somber. "Did you try to commit suicide?"

Oh, God, why couldn't he give it a rest?

"No." I sucked in a deep breath. "Jaime, please. I can't go there with you yet." *And maybe never.*

"Okay, Gloria, I get it. You can't completely trust me. Maybe one day you will."

I absorbed his words. My wishful thinking hoped he was right. Calming myself with another deep breath, I moved away from the past and jumped into the future.

"So, Mr. Imagination, how do you envision us having a long distance relationship?" With three thousand miles separating us, it wasn't going to be easy.

He toyed with my braid again. "Like I always say, where there's a will, there's a way. I'm thinking we shoot the Gloria's Secret campaign out here in some decadent Beverly Hills or Hancock Park mansion. I can also fly out here on weekends. In between, I expect to Skype you regularly. Not just in your office. I want you to take your laptop or tablet to bed every night. I'm going to go to sleep with you and wake up to you every day."

The thought of having both virtual good-night and wake-up sex with my sexy, creative beast on a daily basis sent hot tingles to my already zinging core.

"And what about Victor?" I was pushing hard for answers.

"Fuck the bastard. He won't be around." I could feel every muscle in his body contract.

Before I could probe further, his cell phone rang. With his free arm, he reached for it. It was in a pocket of his white linen pants. He put the phone to his ear and listened.

His mouth twitched. "Yeah, babe, I haven't forgotten. I'll see you there soon." With that, he ended the call and sat up, lifting me up with him. He glanced down at his Rolex.

"Gloria, I've got to go. I have to meet with a client."

"That client you call babe?" My tone was sharp. I needed to know.

"Yeah, that one. Stop worrying about her. It's a very important meeting, but she's nothing to me." His brows furrowed and his face tensed. "Please trust me, Gloria."

I still didn't know whether to believe him. *Or* trust him. I fidgeted with my *toi et moi* ring. This was not the way to enter into a relationship.

"No problem. I've got a meeting too." *Vivien.*

My blood was boiling. He sensed my unease. Playing with my disheveled braid, he swept the tip of it across my lower lip. "Listen, angel, I want you to call me around seven thirty. If the meeting with my client goes well and I get the information I need, we can have dinner."

I did the math in my head. That would give me just enough time to have drinks with Vivien and then meet him; The Ivy was just a two minute drive to Shutters, if that, in fact, was where he was meeting his client. There was no need for him to know about my plans, and Vivien was one name that I wanted to keep out of our relationship. That and Victor's.

He lifted me to my feet. The sun, a great big orange ball of fire, was setting into the ocean. It must have been close to five; I'd lost track of time. Reality set back in. It was time to face the storm and return to my office.

We both hastily donned our clothes. I pivoted toward the car, but before I could take a step, he grabbed me by the waist, flipped me around, and sent me orbiting with another long, lingering passionate kiss. I didn't want it to end. In my heart, I hoped he'd be free for dinner...and save me for dessert. And tell me he loved me.

Chapter 9

JAIME MANAGED TO GET ME back to my office just in time for me to change back into my suit and meet Vivien at The Ivy. Truthfully, I was wiped out from the day's events and wanted to go back to my condo and rest up, just in case Jaime was free for dinner. I thought about canceling drinks and even called Vivien on her cell phone. It rang several times and then went straight to her voice mail. Damn it! I couldn't stand her up. I was stuck having drinks with her. Just before I left my office, I checked my e-mails and messages on my cell phone, which I'd left behind while on my excursion with Jaime. Fuck! Almost all of them were from Victor. I played the first one. The tone of his voice was menacing. "Where the hell are you, Gloria? You're not in your office, and you're not picking up your cell. Call me!" There were several more of these messages, each one angrier than the one before, as well as numerous all-caps shouty e-mails and texts. Screw him! Let him stew. I threw my cell phone into my purse, and with my briefcase in my other hand, I waltzed out of my office, lightheaded with the thought of possibly seeing Jaime later.

On my way out of the building, I passed by numerous employees. With bright smiles, they bid me good night; some even mentioned how awesome my speech was today. A warm feeling radiated throughout me. I was blessed to have so many wonderful employees. They worked long hours and were dedicated to their jobs. And they were dedicated to me. The thought of losing them sent a ripple of sadness through me. I told myself, it was not going to happen. I wasn't very convincing.

I made it to The Ivy at exactly six thirty. The LA rush hour traffic was the only thing I couldn't take about this city. It was insane. Fifteen years ago when I'd moved to The City of Angels, it took only twenty minutes to get from place to place. Now, it took forty—if you were lucky. Tonight I was lucky.

I left my Porsche with the valet outside the restaurant, tipping the attendant extra to keep it parked nearby. "Time equals money," I always preached, and with the stock crisis, every minute counted. I strode into the popular restaurant and headed straight to the tropical-themed bar. It was already packed with attractive men and women, enjoying an after-work drink or waiting for a table to dine. One of my favorite songs, Leona Lewis's "Bleeding Love," was playing in the background. My eyes scanned the area. Vivien, not known for her punctuality, was nowhere to be found. I immediately called her on my cell phone, wanting to know her whereabouts. No answer. I left her a message, asking to call or text me with her estimated time of arrival. And then another thought crossed my mind. Perhaps, she had reserved a table inside the restaurant. I headed back to the hostess holding court near the entrance.

"Could you please tell me if Vivien Holden has a reservation for two at six thirty?" I asked.

Standing behind a podium, the bubbly blonde, for sure a young, aspiring actress with her bombshell looks, scanned her reservations log. Her face brightened. "Yes!" She gazed up at me. "Are you, by chance, Ms. Long?"

I nodded. "Yes."

"Follow me," she said with a wide smile. "Ms. Holden is expecting you."

Keeping up with her, I had to say I was impressed that Vivien had thought ahead and made a table reservation. Noisy bars with horny singles were just not my thing.

"She's seated in the corner table to the right," said the hostess as we wove through the busy restaurant.

My eyes darted in that direction and my heart dropped to the floor.

Sure enough, there was Vivien, all dolled up. And cozied up next to her was a drop dead handsome man with his lips latched onto hers in a passionate embrace. Jaime Zander!

I stood paralyzed in shock. Every ounce of blood drained from my system. A bullet had once almost tore through my heart. This time it was as if it didn't miss. The excruciating pain didn't give rage a chance.

"Are you okay?" asked the hostess.

At first, I couldn't get my mouth to move; it hung open but it was like my jaw was wired shut. I fortified myself with a deep painful breath, forcing reason and movement back into my being. "Yes," I stuttered. "I can take it from here."

The hostess, oblivious to the turmoil raging

inside me, told me to enjoy my evening and skirted away.

Run, don't walk, my inner voice urged. Which way? Out the door? My legs were buried in cement. I still couldn't get them to move.

Then, without warning, a sudden rush of adrenaline surged inside me. I stormed up to them. They were still in a heated embrace.

"Is this your business client?" I grinded out the words as burning tears sprung to my eyes.

The familiar sound of my voice stopped Jaime in his tracks. He abruptly jerked away from Vivien and gazed up at me. His face was drained of color, and his eyes were as round as two blue marbles. "Jesus fucking Christ!" he gasped in shock.

"Fuck you!" I screamed back at him.

Vivien flung her head back and raked her fingers through her perfectly blown Cleopatra-styled hair. Some doctor's appointment—she'd spent the afternoon beautifying for her hot date. She was perfectly made up, and her tight little red dress practically still had the price tag on it. A wicked, triumphant smile flitted across her face. "So nice to see you, Gloria. Do you want to join us? Jaime was just telling me about all the good ideas he has to get Gloria's Secret back on track."

My eyes lanced into him. He remained speechless. Hurt and rage continued to battle for the prize of my broken heart. How could have I fallen for him? Put everything I had into him? Believed what he'd told me only a few hours ago? Let myself think there was a future with him? Suddenly, I felt god damn fucking stupid. I'd been played. Played by that vixen bitch Vivien, who cleverly lured me here, and used by a bastard sex god who used his cock to get to me and win my account. I'd been deceived. Totally, terribly deceived.

Jaime attempted to say something. "Gloria, I had no idea—"

I cut him off. "Take your fucking ring back. There is no *toi et moi*!" Burning now with rage, I tore the ring off my middle finger and hurled it at him. It bounced off his rock-hard chest and landed with a loud ping somewhere on the floor. My shaking finger stung like hell. I glanced down at it. Fuck. I'd torn off a sizeable chunk of skin on my knuckle. It was raw and bleeding.

"Ooh, that must hurt," cooed Vivien.

My finger throbbed, but it was nothing compared to the throbbing in my heart.

Alarmed, Jaime jumped to his feet and reached for my hand. "Let me see your finger."

I jerked my hand away from him. "Don't touch me!" I hissed.

I snatched a clean napkin off the table and wrapped it around the wound. With tears scorching down my face, I raced out of the restaurant.

Thank goodness, I'd given the valet an extra ten bucks to keep my car parked nearby. It was still sitting in front of the restaurant. The cool ocean breeze sent goose bumps all over me.

"That's my car," I told one of the attendants, pointing to the black Porsche with my good hand. My voice was hurried. Panicked.

"The key's inside." Catching sight of the now bloodstained napkin wrapped around my other hand, he sensed my urgency.

Without wasting a second, I stepped off the curb and rounded my car to the driver's side door. As I gripped the cold metal handle with my good hand, I felt two powerful hands clutch my waist. They spun me around, and I was face-to-face with the man I never wanted to see again. Jaime Zander.

"Let go of me, you bastard!" I tried to squirm away, but it was futile. He held on to me too firmly.

His intense denim blues gazed into my wretched, watering eyes. "Gloria, it's not what you think. You don't understand. Please. You *have* to trust me."

"Trust you? You want me to trust you?" *God fucking damn it.* "I *did* trust you. I let you fuck me till I fell apart. I just wasn't counting on you to make my heart fall apart so soon." My nostrils flared as I sobbed. "You and Vivien belong together."

Desperation swept over his face. "No, I belong with you, angel."

"Don't ever call me that!" Tears flocked my eyes. I turned my head away from him. With one hand, he clenched my jaw, forcing me to look his way. I resisted.

"Stop it! You're hurting me."

He immediately let go, and I turned on my own to face him.

His eyes bore into mine, but his voice was soft and repentant. "I'm sorry, angel. I've never meant to hurt you."

"Well, you could have fooled me." Tears streamed down my face. I was worn out, physically and emotionally. I pleaded with him one more time: "Please. Let. Me. Go."

To my relief, he released me and stepped back. He lowered his long-lashed eyes. "I'm sorry, angel. I wish I could explain."

"There's nothing to explain. Actions speak louder than words." With that, I clambered into the car, slamming the door behind me. I frantically locked it before he could yank it open. Cursing, he punched the roof as I threw the sports car into first gear. Fuck him! Without another look at him, I floored the gas pedal and peeled away with an ear-piercing screech.

My hands shook on the steering wheel, and tears blinded my vision as I turned right off Ocean Avenue onto Wilshire Boulevard. Thank god, it was just one short, straight line back to my condo. My finger throbbed, and my heart was running a marathon with despair at the finish line. How could I have let this man get to me? How could I have been so spineless, so gullible? So stupid? I hated Jaime. I hated Vivien. But most of all, I hated myself.

The sound of a loud horn blared in my ears. Distraught and distracted, I ran a red light and narrowly missed being hit. Shit. I was totally out of control. Silently, I prayed I wouldn't get into an accident. In my condition, I wasn't meant to be on the road. *Focus, Gloria, focus!* My face wet with tears and my emotions raging like a hurricane, I somehow managed to make it to my high-rise building. Coming to a skidding stop, I left the car with the valet and dashed past the doorman to the elevator before he could greet me. I pounded the call button and headed straight into the arms of the one person in the world I *could* trust. Kevin Riley.

Kevin's condo was one floor below mine. While not as

big as my two-story penthouse, it was nonetheless spacious and enjoyed views of the city all around. It was impeccably furnished with high-end Italian furniture that complimented framed black and white photographs, mostly of beautiful men, on the walls.

"Holy shit, Glorious. What's wrong?" he gasped at the sight of me. With my tear-streaked face, bloodshot eyes, and bloody bandaged hand, I must have been a sorrowful sight. I kicked off my heels at the entrance and let myself fall into him, burying my head on his chest. After letting me sob like that for several long minutes, he wrapped a comforting arm around me and ushered me into his apartment. "Tell me everything."

I collapsed into one of his comfy cream leather club chairs, folding my good hand over the other with the makeshift bandage. Though I thought the bleeding had stopped, my finger throbbed more than ever. I continued to cry ugly tears. "Oh, Kev, I caught Jaime with Vivien. He told me in Paris there was nothing between them. He lied to me! He was all over her." I launched into the day's events—of how Jaime had driven me to his seaside property and made a commitment to me and of how Vivien had set me up to prove he was a two-timing prick.

Reddening with rage, Kevin slammed his fist onto the arm of the chair; his temper was equal to Jaime's. "Fucking Vivien!"

"No, not fucking Vivien. Fucking bastard. Stupid me. It's probably better I found out now that he was a cheating asshole and was just using me."

I lifted my good hand to wipe my tears. Kevin's eyes immediately took hold of the bloodstained napkin wrapped around the other on my lap. Alarm swept over him.

"Glorious, what did you do to your hand?"

I slowly unwrapped the napkin. The damaged finger made my whole hand tremble, the ugly wound red and raw. "I tore off my skin when I tore off his ring."

Though not adverse to blood, Kevin scrunched up his face. "Sheesh, that looks really nasty." He rose from the couch. "Don't move. I'm going to patch it up."

A faint but grateful smile spread across my tear-soaked face. As he sauntered off, I thought about how lucky I was to have him in my life. My mind flashed back to our final days in Brighton Beach... hiding out in the small one-bedroom apartment we shared...Kevin taking care of me as I lay feverishly in his bed with an infected bullet wound...falling in and out of consciousness...waking to find him cleaning the wound and changing the dressing while my body shook from pain and fever. He nursed me back to health, with the help of a local doctor whose children he'd once tutored, and masterminded our escape. Our new life. Yes, Kevin was the only person I could trust in the world.

One short minute later, he was back with first aid—clutching a bottle of peroxide, some cotton balls, and a box of Gloria's Secret adhesive bandages in his hands.

He lowered himself onto the arm of the chair, laying out the first aid supplies next to him. He grabbed a cotton ball and soaked it with the peroxide.

"Glorious, this is going to sting," he warned as he gently dabbed it on my raw, bloody wound. No shit.

I winced. He dabbed it again and then pulled out a wide adhesive bandage from the box of Gloria's Secret bandages. Earlier in the year, we had made a licensing deal with a major pharmaceutical company. Our focus group research had shown that single women loved to use the shiny white Band-Aids with our signature bright pink heart to hide hickies while moms reported that their little girls loved them to cover up boo-boos. Our first licensing deal had turned out to be a huge success.

"Try to hold your finger steady." I watched as Kevin peeled off the paper wrapping and then circled the bandage around my ravaged knuckle. The signature pink heart sat just above where two entwining diamond hearts had once been. If only there was a bandage big enough to cover my aching heart. Jaime had cut it open, and it kept on bleeding tears.

Kevin admired his handiwork. "Try not bend your finger or get it wet while it heals."

I nodded. "Thanks, Kev," I sniffled and lightly kissed him on the cheek.

"Do you want to stay over?" he asked. "Or want me to come up?"

I quirked another small smile. "Thanks for the offer, but I think I need some time alone to think things through." There was so much to think about—everything in my life was going so wrong. At the top of my list was the future of Gloria's Secret, and my broken heart was not going to make dealing with it easier.

I passed on a glass of wine and slogged one floor up to my condo. I was barely one foot inside it when the intercom buzzer sounded. I pressed the button on the wall by the door, careful not to use my bandaged finger.

It was Walter, the kindly sixty-five-year-old doorman. "Ms. Long, there's a gentleman by the name of Jaime Zander here to see you," I heard him say through the speaker. My heart skipped a beat and my body shook. I quickly bolt-locked my door. "Tell him I don't want to see him."

"He's insistent on seeing you."

"Tell him to go away." My voice was quivering.

The next voice I heard was not the doorman's. It was Jaime's. "Jesus fucking Christ, Gloria, let me up!"

"Go away," I pleaded, my voice watery.

Walter: "Ms. Long, do you want me to call security?"

"Fuck security!" I heard Jaime growl. Shit! I hoped he wasn't going to do in the poor, soon-to-retire doorman. With his red-hot temper and brutal strength, it was a possibility. I shuddered.

Walter's voice cracked with panic. "Ms. Long, he's coming up. I couldn't stop him. I'm calling security now."

"No, Walter. It's okay. Don't call security."

A combination of dread and despair filled me. My heart pounded and tears fell from my eyes. I sagged down against the door into a crouching position. There was a loud pounding on the other side. Jaime.

"Gloria, let me in!"

"Go away!"

He pounded harder. "God damn it, Gloria. Open. The. Door."

"No!" I sobbed.

"Just do it!" He gave the door a hard kick—so hard I could feel the vibration against my back.

"I swear I'm going to kick the door down if you don't open up." He began to frantically kick the door. I painfully felt each angry kick.

"Stop it!" I choked. "I'm going to call 911 if you don't leave." Of course, I wasn't.

He gave the door another loud, hard kick. "Fuck you, Gloria. You're not the only one who can fall apart." And then the pounding, screaming, and kicking stopped. He was gone. Heaving sobs wracked my body. I buried my head between my knees and just let the tears fall. I had won the battle, but victory eluded me. I forced myself to get up and stumbled to the window that overlooked Wilshire Boulevard. Gazing down at the busy street below through my tears, I watched Jaime Zander peel away in his Thunderbird convertible. I rubbed my throbbing finger as he raced down the boulevard and disappeared. Pain ripped through my body. My heart was still bleeding tears.

Chapter 10

M Y SNOOZE ALARM RANG AT six a.m. I pulled the covers over my eyes. I didn't want to get out of bed. There was only one word to describe how I felt—sick. Very, very sick. My eyes stung from crying; a thick, painful lump in my throat made it almost impossible to swallow, and waves of nausea brushed against my chest. Madame Paulette had once said, "Love *eez* a disease for which there *eez* no cure." I shuddered—were these the symptoms? Was this how I was going to feel the rest of my life?

Yes, Jaime fucking Zander had broken my heart. He had asked for my trust—and my love—and all the while, he was deceiving me. Once the player, always the player. The heart-wrenching pain I felt from his deceit was in many ways worse than that of a bullet wound. It hurt physically *and* emotionally. As much as I willed the image of his beautiful face out of mind, it wouldn't go away. Memories of all the good times we had together danced in my head and brought a rush of fresh tears to my eyes. I couldn't stop reliving our most recent passionate encounter overlooking the Pacific Ocean. But each time I replayed it, the divine feeling of his fullness inside me succumbed to the excruciating emptiness I now felt in my heart.

The alarm went off again, and I made my first executive decision of the day. Fuck it! I wasn't going into my office—at least not this morning. Yes, I felt sick but that hadn't stopped me before. The truth... I couldn't face Vivien. The image of that vixen kissing Jaime flooded my head and made me shiver. If only I could fire her, but that wasn't an option. Her type of betrayal wasn't on the list of Human Resources' causes for job termination. And there was always Daddy to protect her tight little ass.

With my burning eyes still closed, I forced Jaime to the back of my mind and focused on what I had to do today. To the best of my knowledge, I didn't have any major meetings—except that dreaded lunch with Victor at noon to meet a potential business partner. I could work from home and then meet him at the Polo Lounge. Depending on how I felt after lunch, I would decide whether to go into my office. And then I remembered...

Tonight was my big night—I was being honored at the Beverly Hilton for the charitable work I'd done as the founder and chief supporter of Girls Like Us. I'd been so looking forward to this event but now I dreaded it. Oh, God. How was I going to get it together? Face a crowd of over a thousand people? I hadn't even written my speech. Maybe, I'd just wing it—that is, if I made it through the day.

Sliding down the covers, I reached for my cell phone on my night table. I'd put the ringtone on mute before crawling into bed last night, not having the strength or desire to deal with anything or anyone. There were thirty missed calls—all of them from Jaime. As fast as I could, I deleted all his messages, not wanting to hear his voice. My middle finger still throbbed like my heart. Tears stung my eyes. I had cried myself to sleep so hard, it was hard to believe I still had tears to shed.

Listlessly, I entered Kevin's seven-digit phone number on the touch screen; I knew it by heart, and it was way easier to reach him this way than to scroll down my long list of contacts. He picked up on the first ring.

"Morning Glory, how are you feeling?"

"Like crap." Kevin was the one person from whom I could never hide things, and just from my painfully hoarse voice, he would be able to detect my deplorable state of being. Shit! How was I possibly going to give a speech tonight when I could barely talk?

"You sound awful. Is there anything I can do?"

"Yeah, Kev, would you hold things down at the office. I'm not coming in...at least this morning."

"You've got it."

"Thanks."

"Do you want me to cancel tonight's gala?" There was hesitancy in his voice.

Kevin, my head of Public Relations, had spent months carefully planning the Beverly Hilton event; he had been looking forward to it as much as I had. I gulped a breath of air. As much as I wished I could call it off—hell, I was in no mood to get an award and be all smiley-faced—I couldn't. Important people from all over the country had flown in for the $1000 per ticket, Oprah-hosted fundraiser, including celebrities and politicians as well as one hundred underprivileged young girls who were likely squeeing about getting princess makeovers, courtesy of me, and attending their first-ever black tie event. I had also bought tables for many of our employees.

"No, Kev. I can't do that. I'll be there."

Kevin proceeded to fill me in on the latest stock crisis news. It was not good. Rumors all over Wall Street were circulating that the Board of Directors was going to ask me to resign. This day was quickly going from bad to worse. Reality stabbed at me. By tonight, I might even be introduced as the "former CEO of Gloria's Secret."

I told Kevin to keep me posted of any new developments and then ended the call with an exchange of "I love you." He always had been and always would be there for me. Our last words whirled around in my head. *I love you.* Jaime and I had never uttered these three words nor would we ever. My heart sunk lower as if lower were possible.

As much as I wished I could stay in bed all day with the covers over my head, I was still, at least for the moment, CEO of Gloria's Secret, and I couldn't eschew my responsibilities. I forced myself to roll out of the bed and stumbled to the bathroom. I glimpsed my reflection in the mirror. I looked every bit the train wreck I was. My duo-colored eyes were bloodshot and swollen; my skin pasty, and my long braid was a disheveled mess. I immediately brushed my teeth just to get the taste of something fresh in my system. It helped, the minty toothpaste revitalizing me a little. What I really needed was a shower.

Despite Kevin's urging not to get my bandaged

finger wet, I let the hot water pound on my flesh, sparing no inch of me; it stung my finger. With a large soapy sponge, I washed every part of my body, but I couldn't wash the painful memory of Jaime Zander away. It was moreover impossible not to think about the sensuous times we'd showered together. Tearfully, I circled the scar that never let me forget that my past was real. Beneath that scar, there was a new one that could only be felt, not seen. It was the scar on my heart that Jaime Zander had left behind. Madame Paulette had once told me that the scars you can't see are the hardest to heal. I wondered—do they ever?

Stepping out of the shower, I towel dried myself with a soft white bath sheet and then donned my oversized Gloria's Secret robe. The softness of the velvety terry cloth against my skin was comforting. Standing before the mirror, I was pleased to see that the shower had improved my reflection a bit. My skin again had a fresh glow, and while my eyes still had a few ugly red spider lines, they were no longer red balls of fire. I spritzed myself with a little GS cologne and then braided my hair. My throbbing stiff middle finger made weaving my long locks difficult. The almost waist-length braid was definitely not my best. After securing the wispy ends with an elastic, I decided to take a look-see at my finger. I peeled off the wet bandage and grimaced. My knuckle looked gruesome. It was still raw, inflamed, and puffy. I should have heeded Kevin's advice. This was definitely the kind of wound that was going to get worse before it got better. I opened my medicine cabinet, pulled out my own box of Gloria's Secret bandages, and re-covered it. I stared at the bright pink heart in the center of the bandage that sat smack on my torn flesh. Thoughts of Jaime flew into my head...that cocky smile, those beautiful denim blue eyes, all those crazy sexual encounters. He had unleashed a hidden power inside me and made me feel like beautiful goddess. He'd even saved my life! Fresh tears were verging. God fucking damn it! Confession: As much as I loathed him, I still loved him. Fuck love. It hurt. My finger would eventually heal, but I wasn't sure about my heart. As I lumbered out of the bathroom and headed to my desk, I was no longer sure if it was better to have loved and lost than never to have loved at all. By the time I was slumped over my computer, I was sorry that I'd ever met Jaime Zander.

Occupying myself with my e-mails didn't help. There were at least fifty e-mails from Jaime, each one begging me to call, text, or e-mail him back in the subject line. In one swoop, I deleted all of them. My sorrow morphed into rage. I wasn't going to let him get the time of day with me. Rules are made to be broken, he had said, and so were contracts. Screw a deal is a deal! I immediately fired off an e-mail to Business Affairs, asking if we had signed a contract with ZAP! and if we did, to find a way to get out of it. Before I could hit send, my intercom buzzed. My heart jumped. Shit! Could it be him?

I jogged downstairs and sprinted to the intercom. I pressed the button. Through the speaker, Jules, our daytime doorman, piped that there was a man here to see me.

My heart thudded; I cut him off. "What does he look like?"

"I'd say he's about six-foot three—*Thud!*—has

longish brown hair—*Thud!*—blue eyes—*Thud!*—and he's probably in his sixties—*Phew!* And he's got a delivery for you."

"Send him up," I said with a sigh of relief. Okay. Confession: I was disappointed. I perversely wished it had been Jaime. What was wrong with me?

Five minutes later, the deliveryman was at my door. I unbolted the lock and gaped. Tucked in his arms were three crystal vases, each filled with a dozen magnificent red roses. They were just like the ones Jaime had bought me in Paris. My heart teetered between melting with joy and exploding with rage. I almost told the man to take them back from wherever they came but ultimately told him to place the vases on the entryway console. The apartment instantly filled up with their heavenly scent. Once the deliveryman was gone, I ripped open the small envelope that was clipped to a plastic holder planted among the roses. There was a handwritten note inside, the penmanship black and bold. I shook as I read it.

Angel~
Please trust me.
Je t'aime.
~Jaime

I crumpled the note in my trembling hand. Tears seared my eyes. Why was he doing this to me? Was this the beautiful bastard's latest ploy to make me fall apart? If it was, he was succeeding. My emotions were in turmoil, flying out of control. One by one, I hurled the vases onto the white marble floor. Fuck you, Jaime Zander! *SMASH! SMASH! SMASH!* They were as shattered as my heart. Tears spilled into the water that was drowning the now tattered, scattered roses. I was too much of an emotional wreck to clean up the mess. In a tailspin, I ran back upstairs to my computer and sent my e-mail off to Business Affairs. Whatever it took, Jaime Zander needed to be out of my life. I shut down my computer, set my alarm clock to 11:00, muted all my phones, and then did something I hadn't done in a very long time. I sat down on the carpet, crossed my legs, and closed my eyes. I meditated.

At exactly eleven a.m., the loud ring of my alarm clock brought me out of my deep meditation. I slowly peeled open my eyes, took a deep inhale, and brought awareness back into my body. I felt empowered. Back in control. There was no Jaime Zander lurking in my head.

I rose to my feet and marched over to my lingerie commode, selecting my favorite, most uplifting black lace bra, panties, garter, and silk stockings. Fifteen minutes later, I was again dressed for success in my killer Louboutins and the Dior dress that I'd worn to Madame Paulette's funeral. My little black mourning dress. In no mood to drive, I called my driver Tyrone and told him to meet me downstairs at 11:30. Grabbing my purse, I scurried out the door, ready to meet Victor Holden head on. I was not going to let him take me down.

Chapter 11

THE LEGENDARY PINK BEVERLY HILLS Hotel was located a few miles from my condo on Sunset Boulevard. Tyrone let me out at the entrance. A long-legged valet instantly ran up to the car and opened the passenger door.

"Good afternoon, Ms. Long. Welcome back."

I was quite a fixture at the Beverly Hills Hotel, meeting numerous vendors and reporters here, especially for breakfast at the famed Polo Lounge. And this was, of course, where Victor Holden held all his business meetings. It was a favorite celebrity and power mogul hangout.

As I stepped out of the Range Rover, I told Ty to wait for me nearby. That I hoped to be done with Victor and whomever else I was meeting by two o'clock. He obliged with a big smile.

Passing through the famous pink and green Art Deco-inspired lobby, I strutted to the Polo Lounge located to the rear. My long-stepped stride was a blend of sexy confidence and arrogance, one that had heads turning. Once inside the Polo Lounge, I spotted Victor immediately. Dressed in one of his classic three-piece gray suits, he was seated at his favorite green leather corner booth in the dimly lit front room. A tumbler was in his hand. His afternoon bourbon. When I strode up to his table, he rose, his lecherous eyes leering at my body from head to toe.

"Why, darling, I must say you are holding up quite well given what you must be going through." He grasped my hand and put it to his lips.

I so wanted one of those antiseptic wipes to wash off his slimy kiss. I mentally sneered at him as I sidled into the booth until I was seated in the middle. I acted cool, calm, and collected. Like the Forbes power woman I was.

"Thank you, Victor. I'm confident that the stock crisis is just a little glitch, and we'll be back on track shortly. The prototype for the vibrator came in, and I must say it exceeded my expectations." I felt a throb between my legs. *Oh, Jaime!*

"That's good to hear." A smug smile curved on his lips. "So, Gloria, have you reconsidered my offer?"

I flinched. Under the table, his free hand ran up and down my thigh. *Pig!* I kept a poker face.

"Victor, the only thing I've focused on is the stock crisis." *That and the affair your slut for a daughter is having with Jaime Zander.* Inwardly shuddering, I wondered if he knew about it—or was even aware of Vivien's perverted history with her stepbrother.

His steely eyes narrowed. "Are you still seeing Jaime Zander?"

The mention of his name unhinged me but I acted calm. "No, I'm not seeing your *stepson.*"

At the word "stepson," Victor flinched. His hand flew off my thigh. He was taken aback and for sure knew I was aware of his violent past. Like a snake, it was time to strike. I took a deep breath before showing my fangs and asking, "Victor, why were you the first to sell off so many shares when you knew business was solid, in fact, poised for growth?"

My question caught him off guard. He twitched and gulped his bourbon. Slamming the tumbler onto the table, his eyes darted to the left. "Ah, here comes our meeting."

My gaze followed his. Lumbering toward us was a stocky man wearing a long black trench coat, the collar curled up, and a wide brimmed hat that obscured his face. There was something déjà-vu about him. Where had I seen him before? I racked my brain. *Think, Gloria, think.* And then it hit me— in the lobby of The Intercontinental Hotel in Paris just after checking in.

The man stopped at our table and removed his hat. I almost shit my panties. I knew this man! It was a face I'd never forget! The face of a monster!

"Gloria, I'd like you to meet..."

Boris Borofsky! I wasn't sure if I even heard Victor say his name. For a brief second, my heart stopped beating. Everything inside me died. Then my heart beat into a frenzy.

Victor continued. "He owns a chain of very successful international sex clubs. We met in Paris and thought there might be a natural synergy between his enterprise and Gloria's Secret. An opportunity to get our products into his many clubs around the world. Perhaps set up Gloria's Secret boutiques inside them and create an exclusive BDSM product line."

Still standing, Boris's eyes, the color of pink quartz, clashed with mine. I felt myself turning as white as a ghost. If only I were a ghost and could make myself invisible. I tried hard to steady my right hand as I offered it to him to shake. His stubby, thick-skinned fingers entwined mine, his grip so hard I almost winced. My bandaged finger throbbed with pain as the horrific memory of these fingers wrapped around my neck threatened to undo me.

"A pleasure to meet you, Ms. Long," he said in his unforgettable, thickly accented husky voice. Still squeezing my hand, he gazed into my duo-colored eyes. His white-lashed pink eyes narrowed into razor blades. "You have fascinating eyes, Ms. Long. It is rare to meet someone who has *vun* blue eye and *vun* brown *vun.*"

Oh, God! Did he recognize me? It was hard to tell because he was maintaining his cool. I twitched a smile and thanked him.

"I never forget a beautiful face. Have we met before?"

Every hair on my body bristled. "No, I'm sure we've never met," I stammered. *Stay calm, Gloria! Don't let him hear your heart thundering.*

"Are you sure we never met several years back in New York?" His voice was growing more ominous by the second.

Fuck! He knew! He knew who I was! "Yes, I'm sure," I managed with a nervous smile.

He smiled coyly. "You must be right. It *vould* be hard to forget an albino freak like me."

I inwardly shivered. I now wasn't sure if he was putting me on or believed me.

He thudded around the table and sat down next to me. My eyes fixed on him. He was completely bald now and paunchy, and despite obvious plastic surgery, the bullet hole scars that bracketed his fat chalky lips made him even more hideous than he already was.

A waiter came by to take our drink order. Another bourbon for Victor, a Stoli straight up for Boris, and a sparkling water for me. I couldn't let alcohol cloud my thinking.

"Cheers!" said Victor when the drinks arrived. "To our future together."

Fuck! I wasn't sure I was going to have a future as I clinked glasses with Victor, who was back to manhandling me under the table, and with Boris, who was mentally stabbing me in my gut. He eyed my bandaged finger.

"*Vhat* happened to your finger, my beauty?" His sinister voice was going down a path.

I twitched another skittish smile. Inside, every nerve ending was on edge. I could barely breathe. "It's nothing. Just a minor scrape."

He leaned in close to me, his quartz eyes burning another hole into my chest. "Do you *vant* to know *vhat* happened to my face? Most people do. Although I bet you can guess." He snarled at me. "Scars have the power to remind us that our pasts are real, don't they, Ms. Long?"

My heart was beating so fast I thought it would ricochet out of my chest. Sweat poured from behind my knees as nausea rose to my chest. Grabbing my bag, I leaped up.

"Excuse me, I'll be right back. I need to use the restroom." I was going to throw up any minute.

Boris forcefully grabbed my braid, holding me back.

"Hurry back, Gloria. We have business to discuss."

"I'm looking forward to it," I said, jerking myself free of his grip and losing a clump of hair in the process. Keeping an evil eye on me, Boris stood up and let me out of the booth.

Holding my head high, I walked calmly out of the Polo Lounge, and then, the moment I stepped foot into the hotel lobby, I sprinted to the ladies' room located down a hallway to the left. Yanking open the restroom door, I ran straight into a vacant stall and crouched down on the cold marble floor. Holding back my braid with one hand, I puked my guts out over the toilet. Oh God! How could this be happening? First the stock crash! Then Jaime! And now Boris Borofsky was back in my life! I was in harm's way. Big time! Fuck! What was I going to do?

Only one thing was clear. I had to get out of here as quickly as possible. Away from the man who would, without doubt, seek his revenge. Gloria Long could soon be a goner.

After a quick wash of my hands and rinse of my mouth, I raced to the hotel entrance, calling Tyrone on his cell to meet me there as quickly as possible.

Once outside, I tapped my foot anxiously, waiting for Tyrone to pull up, and stole nervous glances behind me. The hotel, popular with the Hollywood crowd and tourists alike, was bustling, with the valets running back and forth to service guests. My galloping heart jumped into my throat when a red Thunderbird convertible pulled up. Oh my God! Jaime!

He immediately saw me and leaped out of his car,

leaving it for the valet. My already tight stomach balled up into a knot of panic.

"Gloria!" His voice was a breathy blend of surprise and desire that complemented the desperation in his lustful eyes.

"What are you doing here?" I gasped.

"Meeting my real estate agent. And you?"

"Leaving." *Oh, please Tyrone, hurry!*

"Did you get my roses?" Facing me, he gripped my shoulders with his strong hands. I trembled beneath his touch.

"Jaime, let go of me!" *Come on, Tyrone!* My prayer was answered. Ty was heading up the driveway. I would have run downhill to meet him, but I couldn't break free from Jaime.

His piercing blue eyes were fierce on my face. "I'm not letting you go until you answer my question."

"Let go of her," thundered another voice behind me. Boris! "She's all mine." With a painful yank of my braid, he tore me away from Jaime.

"Who the fuck are you?" barked Jaime, his eyes flaring.

Boris growled. "Your worst nightmare."

No, my worst nightmare!

"Fuck off, asswipe!" Jaime growled back at him.

Boris didn't know whom he was dealing with. And didn't see it coming. I ducked just in time as Jaime thrust a clenched fist into Boris's ugly face and sent him reeling to the ground. Blood poured out of his bulbous nose and trickled over his hideous scars. A split-second later, Tyrone pulled up. Without waiting for a valet attendant to assist me, I jumped into the Rover and slammed the passenger door shut. Thank God, it automatically locked because Jaime was one step behind me.

Frantically, he tried to yank it open. My eyes held his for a long second and then turned away. Desperate and frustrated, he banged at the tinted window with both fists. "Fucking open up, Gloria!"

Battling tears, I kept my head so that is was facing straight ahead. "Floor it, Ty."

"You got it, Ms. Long." The SUV peeled off from the curb with a screech and a cloud of smoke. I glanced back to see Jaime running after us at hell-bent speed. He had no chance. The car zoomed down Sunset, leaving him in the dust behind.

"Where to, Ms. Long?"

My head was spinning. "I don't know," I murmured as I called Kevin's cell.

It rang and rang. *Pick up, Kev! Please pick up!* Finally, on the fifth ring, I heard the voice I so needed to hear.

"Oh, Kev! I'm in deep shit!" My voice was shaking.

"I know. Victor secretly met with the Board this morning and convinced them to ask you to resign by the end of the week. I'm sorry, Glorious." He let out a defeated sigh.

His words went in one ear and out the other. My position at Gloria's Secret didn't matter anymore. Nothing mattered anymore. Not Victor, not Vivien, and not even Jaime Zander.

"Oh, Kev. It's something way worse!"

"What are you talking about? Shit, Glorious, are you ill?"

"Boris Borofsky's here, and I'm positive he recognized me." The words flew out of my mouth.

Kevin was shocked into silence. One word ended it: "Fuck!"

"What should we do?"

"Hurry back to your apartment and start packing. I'll meet you there in fifteen minutes."

I was randomly throwing anything I could get my hands on quickly into a large suitcase on my bed when I heard footsteps running up the sweeping stairs. Kevin! He was the only one who had keys to my condo and could access it. I ran into his arms as soon I set eyes on him.

"Oh, Kev, what am I going to do?"

"I've arranged for the corporate jet to secretly take us out of the country this evening."

Us? "You're coming with me?"

"Glorious, we're in this together. I could never leave you."

So, we were going to be on the run again from the Russian monster. Fugitives. A tear escaped Kevin's eye. It was rare for him to cry.

"Kev, what's the matter?" My voice was frantic. I needed him more than ever to be strong for me.

He collapsed onto the bed. "Glorious, this is all my fault. I should have never made you steal the money. Boris should be after me, not you. I'm the one who shot him." His body slumped into a heap of despair.

My poor beloved Kevin! He was guilt tripping. I plunked down next to him, and now it was my turn to brush away tears. "Stop it, Kev. You didn't force me to do anything. I agreed to it. You saved my life. If it weren't for you, there would be no Gloria's

Secret. We paid back the scumbag. Look at all we've accomplished together."

Kevin's glazed eyes met mine. "But now, we'll have nothing."

"That's not true. We'll always have each other. We both have money now. We'll build something new. Hey, I'm out of a job anyway, tomorrow."

"But we'll always be on the run. That will never stop."

I squeezed his hand. "As long as I run with you, there's always tomorrow." My own eyes grew teary. "I mean that, Kev."

"Thanks, Glorious." He gave me another hug. We stayed in that embrace for a long minute, until Kevin said, "Come on, let me help you pack."

"Where are we going?"

"For now, Canada. Then we'll figure it out from there."

That meant packing some warm clothes. "What time does the plane leave?"

"At six."

A wave of panic washed over me. "Kev, that's too early. The gala is tonight. I can't miss it. I can't let everyone down, especially those young girls who've been flown in from all over the country to meet me."

"Glorious, its just too fucking dangerous. You're risking your life."

I crossed my arms across my chest and looked him straight in the eye. "There's no negotiation. I'm not going."

Kevin knew I could be stubborn. There was no changing my mind.

He blew out a defeated puff of air. "Fuck. Show me what you're wearing tonight."

Chapter 12

A S AN EXTRA PRECAUTION, WE instructed the doorman on duty to tell anyone who came by looking for us that we weren't in. At exactly five o'clock, we met Tyrone at the back entrance. Kevin was dressed in a slick black tux and sneakers, and me in a stunning one-shoulder gown in signature Gloria's Secret pink; it was custom-made by a local upcoming designer, who owed her success to the Girls Like Us mentoring program. Beneath my gown, I had on a strapless pink satin bra and a matching garter that held up Madame Paulette's lucky silk stockings. I needed all the luck I could get tonight.

Kevin and I sidled into the Range Rover as Tyrone loaded our luggage into the trunk. Sensing our high level of stress, he refrained from asking any questions and silently got behind the wheel. At nine p.m., Kevin and I would be on the corporate jet, secretly heading off to Canada and a new chapter in our broken lives. Gazing down at the bandage that still covered my finger, I felt a deep pang of sadness for everything and everyone I would be leaving behind. In my heart, I longed to say good-bye to all my employees. And to Jaime Zander.

∞

The Beverly Hilton Hotel was a short ten-minute drive from my condo, straight down Wilshire Boulevard, but with the onset of rush hour traffic it took us twice that long. Tyrone dropped us at the front entrance where paparazzi were already gathered. In addition to Oprah hosting the gala, Carrie Underwood was performing, "Nobody Ever Told You," her song about girl power. Numerous celebrities and philanthropists were expected to attend. My charitable organization was one of the most respected in Tinseltown.

Kevin immediately got to work, interacting with the paparazzi and checking the list of VIPs while I was escorted to a small room behind the ballroom stage for hair and makeup. Seated in front of a lit up mirror, I watched as the make up artist and hair stylist, whom we used regularly for our Gloria's Secret catalogue shoots, transformed me into a goddess. I told them I wanted minimal makeup and a simple French braid. Magically, they were able to make the stress I wore on my face go away. As I studied my red-lipped reflection, I saw the image of a young girl with long blond braids pop up next to me in the mirror. Her eyes, one blue, the other brown, gazed proudly at the woman she had become. I held back tears so as not to ruin my eye makeup and wondered if, in reality, I had let the little girl down.

A loud knock at the door made me jump. I was very much on edge, fearing that Boris Borofsky would show up any minute. The words, "Nobody steals from Boris Borofsky," flew into my head as I relived the memory of that horrible night. It had caused me nightmares my entire adult life, and now that nightmare was a reality.

To my relief, it was just Kevin. He was wearing a headset as he always did at big events to communicate with his team. He looked me over from head to toe with a smile of approval.

"You look fabulous, Glorious. The ballroom's practically filled up, so we should probably take seats at our table."

Thanking the stylists, I hooked my arm into Kevin's and let him escort me to our front row table. My eyes drank in the beauty of the vast room, an elegant spectacle of crystal chandeliers and soaring vases of fragrant white roses—Madame Paulette's favorite—on every linen-covered table.

Victor, in a traditional tux, was already seated at the table, with a bourbon, along with several key Gloria's Secret executives. There were two empty seats to the right of him and two to the left. He rose and pulled out the seat on the right that was closest to him, signaling where he wanted me to sit. As much as I didn't want to be anywhere close to the swine, I had no choice. Kevin took the seat next to mine, but just as soon as he sat down, he jumped up to work the room. I'm sure one of the other two seats was for the perpetually late Vivien, but wondered who would occupy the last remaining seat. A terrifying thought crossed my mind—had Victor invited Boris to the gala? I shivered.

Victor's steely eyes bore into mine. "So, Gloria, where the hell did you disappear to this afternoon? I tried to reach you everywhere."

"I had a sudden medical emergency." That wasn't far from the truth. "I'm sorry. I should have let you know."

His eyes flared with fury. "You cost me a valuable piece of business. Boris was furious with you. He wants nothing to do with Gloria's Secret."

I inwardly sighed with relief. That meant there was no way Boris would be showing up here and sitting at our table.

Victor chugged his drink. "You're going to pay for that, Gloria."

I scoffed at him. "Haven't I already? Why didn't you tell me you secretly called a Board meeting and convinced them to ask for my resignation tomorrow?"

"I don't report to you, Gloria." His voice was a blend of ice and contempt.

"And I don't report to you, Victor. I quit."

Victor gaped, but before he could utter a word, a new voice entered the conversation.

"Hello, Daddy." It was Vivien. Dressed in a gold lamé, body-hugging halter dress, that barely covered her melon-sized boobs, and matching six-inch heels, she slithered up to the table. My blood froze over. Like a piece of jewelry, she was dangling on the arm of a man who made my heart stop—Jaime Zander, devastatingly handsome in an elegant tuxedo.

A wicked predatory smile that was meant for me snaked across her over made-up face. Jaime-is-mine was written all over it. My chest tightened painfully.

Jaime's denim blue eyes made contact with mine. I swear, even though he was with Vivien, they lusted only for me. In my highly anxious state, it was probably just my mind playing tricks on me. Or perhaps the bastard was back to playing his cruel head games. One thing, however, couldn't be surer—the physical effect this gorgeous man was having on me. As much as I loathed him, he still took my breath away. My shredded heart hammered against my gown. I should have known he'd be here with Vivien. I took a sip of wine and forced it past the painful lump in my throat.

"Good to see you, Gloria. Congratulations on your award," he said as he pulled out the empty chair next to a shocked Victor for Vivien. There was tension in his voice.

"Thank you," I spluttered as he lowered himself into the last remaining chair. As if I didn't have enough to deal with, his presence was making me sick to my stomach. I imbibed another long swig of wine. Jaime's eyes lingered on my bandaged finger where his ring had once been.

I stole a glance at Victor. He couldn't get his gunmetal eyes off Jaime. He was seething. I knew how much he hated Jaime; he couldn't bear to share the same air as him.

"What the fuck are you doing here, Zander?" he hissed.

"Oh, Daddy..." chimed in Vivien.

"Shut up, Vivien." Fury fueled his voice.

Fearlessly, Jaime met Victor's blazing gaze. "I wouldn't miss this event for the world."

He had come here for me?

"And when you're lovely daughter invited me, I couldn't say no, especially after the great stock tip she gave me."

Victor's eyes narrowed. "What are you talking about?"

A smug smile curled on Jaime's lush lips. "Victor,

at Vivien's suggestion, I'm thinking of buying 50,000 shares of Gloria's Secret stock. We'll get richer together...so I hear."

While Vivien beamed proudly, Victor arched his brows high, causing deep frown lines to set into his forehead. "What the hell did she tell you?" His voice was unusually shaky.

Jaime smiled that dazzling cocky smile. "These two gentlemen can tell you better than I can."

Marching up to us were two burly men, dressed in matching black suits and ties. With their Mr. Clean physiques and identical crew cuts, they looked like they could have been separated at birth. Victor's face blanched.

"Are you Victor Holden?" asked one of the men.

"Yes. I demand to know what this is all about."

"Agents Marshall and Andrews from the FBI," said the other man dryly. In unison, they dug into their inner jacket pockets and whipped out badges.

I exchanged a wide-eyed look with Jaime.

"Victor Holden, you're under arrest for alleged insider trading and stock manipulation." The agent named Marshall issued a warrant and read him his rights.

Victor sprung to his feet. "What are you talking about? You can't prove a thing."

The agent named Andrews dipped a hand into his slacks pocket and pulled out a small recording device. He hit play.

The raspy voice on the machine was familiar. Vivien's. There was chatter and music in the background. I recognized the song—"Undercover Lover." It had ironically been playing at the Walden

Hotel bar when I'd caught Jaime kissing Vivien the first time.

Vivien: "I want to tell you a secret, doll boy."

Jaime: "Babe, I love secrets."

Vivien: "Okay, you've got to promise that you never heard this from me."

Jaime: "Promise."

Vivien: "Remember what I told you at the Touch party? Well, it's true. Daddy's going to short Gloria's Secret, and he's telling all his big investor friends to do the same. The stock is going to drop from an all time high to an all time low and then once that hot line of sex toys is introduced, they're going to buy back all their shares and make a fucking fortune when the stock soars."

Jaime: "When is he going to do that?"

Vivien: "Sometime next week. I'll let you know. You should buy some shares when the price drops."

My eyes, round as saucers, met Jaime's as I gaped with shock. Victor clenched his fists so hard they turned white. A rush of rage bubbled inside me. The hatred I felt toward this man was immeasurable. A fierce scowl replaced my look of shock. The tape played on.

Jaime: "Thanks, Viv, for the hot tip."

Vivien: "You owe me big time... This is what I want... mmm, you like that, don't you?"

My blood curdled at the sound of hungry kisses and moans. They quickly came to an abrupt halt.

Jaime: "Babe, cool it. I don't want Gloria to see us together."

Vivien: (Cackling) "Let the cunt watch. Do exactly as I say."

Jaime: "Lay off, Vivien!"

The wicked dominatrix persevered with her sexual assault and dirty talk, despite Jaime's protest.

Jaime: "Shit! I'll be right back."

That must have been when Jaime spotted me in the lobby of The Walden.

Vivien: "You need to be punished!"

My eyes stayed fixed on Jaime while the FBI agent fast-forwarded the recording, past my tearful exchange with him while he was banging on the town car door and begging me to open it. He paused the tape and then hit play once more. Again, the sound of a chatter and music. Leona Lewis's "Bleeding Love." It had been playing last night at The Ivy.

Vivien: "Daddy's plan is working. But you should wait until Friday to buy the stock."

Jaime: "Why, babe?"

Vivien: "It's going to go lower. Gloria's going to be forced to resign as CEO."

Jaime: "Who's going to take her place?"

Vivien: "Doll boy, you're looking right at her. Now, come to mama."

I was shaking with fury. Agent Andrews clicked off the device, sparing me the pain of having to hear any more. "Have you heard enough, Mr. Holden?"

Victor's face reddened with rage. Vivien, in shock, clapped a hand to her mouth. My eyes bounced back and forth between the two of them and Jaime.

"Oh Daddy, I'm so, so, sorry!" croaked Vivien, her hand still cupped over her mouth.

Victor's lips thinned into a tight angry line and his eyes narrowed with fury. "You stupid, stupid girl. How could you confide in that asshole stepbrother of yours?"

Tears leaked from Vivien's eyes. I glanced at Jaime. Only Mr. Cockiness could nonchalantly shrug his shoulders and roll his eyes. With all this drama and my own to unfold shortly, I seriously didn't know whether to laugh or cry. My mind was a whirling dervish of emotions—shock, rage, and apprehension. My eyes searched the crowd for Kevin. Did he know what was happening? I didn't see him anywhere. Maybe, he was dealing with reporters, trying to prevent Victor's arrest from disrupting the evening.

"Mr. Holden, we advise you to cooperate and not create a scene," said Agent Andrews as he yanked Victor's arms behind his back and handcuffed his wrists. Though still fuming, Victor quietly complied. Shocked eyeballs from other tables turned to him as he was carted away by the two agents. He shot me one last odious look. My eyes shot back a dagger.

Vivien leaped out of her seat. "Don't take my Daddy!" she cried out. She flung herself at her father, desperately clinging to him.

Victor turned to face her, his expression glacial. "Vivien. Let. Go. Of. Me. Now!"

"Oh, Daddy!" Totally defeated, Vivien, in her skintight dress and stilettos, sagged to her knees and sobbed. Her wretched eyes gazed up at Jaime and me. "You fuckers!" she shrieked as her father disappeared into the crowd.

Two husky security guards came to whisk her away. Heaving with sobs, she let them drag her through the ballroom like a sack of potatoes.

I didn't know whether to feel sorry for her or hate her after all she'd done to me. I wondered—was she born a bad seed or had life made her a rotten apple? In the end, I chose to believe that Vivien was as troubled as the girls who went through my mentoring program and hoped she would seek help.

While waiters came around and served the rubber chicken meal that was typical of these kind of events, Jaime Zander moved two seats over into the chair formerly occupied by Victor. I instantly felt the radiating warmth of his body beside me as his muscled thigh brushed against mine. Gently, he tugged at my French braid.

"Gloria." His sultry voice was soft. "You look stunning."

I swallowed hard. My bare arms broke out in goose bumps. Anxiously, I turned to face him. Dressed in black tie, Mr. Elegant was sexier and more gorgeous than ever. His eyes burned into mine, and his breath heated my face.

"Do you trust me?"

I scowled. "You used me to take down Victor. And the little vixen. That's why you wanted the Gloria's Secret account."

He gripped my shoulders and shook me. His voice rose an octave. "Jesus, Gloria. That is so far from the truth. If you remember, you pursued ZAP! and not the other way around."

Suddenly, I felt three feet tall. He was right.

He looked hard into my eyes. "Gloria, the opportunity presented itself. When Vivien leaked what her father was doing at the Touch party in New York, I went straight to the FBI. They were already after him and asked me to fake a relationship with her to extract more incriminating information. I even had to wear this fucking wiretap." He ripped open the buttons of his tux shirt, and yanked it off his beautiful chiseled chest. While I sat there wordless, he tossed it onto the table.

My eyes widened. The wiry contraption with its little black box was just like something out of a TV crime show or movie.

He continued. "And then when I learned that the bastard was trying to bring you down, I couldn't stop." He loosened his grip on my shoulders and then lightly traced my face with his deft fingers. His voice softened. "Angel, I couldn't let that happen to you. It ripped me apart. Do you understand now?"

"Why didn't you tell me?" My voice trembled.

"I was sworn to secrecy."

So, that was Jaime Zander's secret. Though the details of the sting operation were still scant, I understood now that Jaime had used gullible, needy Vivien to bring his nemesis Victor Holden down. And to save my corporate ass. He did it not just for himself, but also for me. My eyes melted into his.

"I'm sorry," I whispered.

"No, angel, I'm the one who's sorry. I never meant to hurt you." He lifted my right hand to his lips and reverently kissed the bandage covering the raw flesh. Under his loving touch, the pain magically faded away. He had once told me that he would never hurt me; I should have believed him.

With his other hand, he tickled the sensitive crook of my neck with the tip of my braid. "I'm going to ask you again. Do you trust me, Gloria?"

I nodded. Tears were brimming in my eyes. How could I have ever doubted this amazing man? This god.

"Good. Then trust me to do this." In a heartbeat, he crushed his lush velvety lips onto mine. My mouth sunk into his. A room full of people may have been watching us, but I was oblivious. At this moment, no one existed but Jaime and me. I never wanted to leave this man. Never! And then reality sunk in as our tongues entwined and did their last dance. In less than an hour, I would be on a plane running away—out of his life forever. Boris Borofsky would ultimately find me wherever I was, and I couldn't put this man, this beautiful, god of a man, who loved and protected me, in harm's way. I had to pay the price for what I'd done without him. Tears leaked out the corners of my clenched eyes. I broke away and turned my head. I could no longer look this man in the face. It hurt too much.

Jaime cradled my head in his soft hands and gently pivoted it so that I was facing him. I kept my heavy eyelids lowered to avoid his gaze. Tears poured freely down my cheeks. Every inch of my body was on fire as he flicked them away with his long, beautiful fingers. "What's the matter, angel? Everything's going to be okay."

"You don't understand." My watery voice was a just above whisper.

"Angel, look at me."

I stole a look at his face. His eyes were fiercely tender.

"The only thing I need to understand is how I feel about you. That night on the plane, when we were in turbulence, I realized that if we went down, I *wanted* to go down with you. Because I couldn't live without you. I need you as much as you need me. When I'm not with you, I'm not whole; I don't function. I can't create. There's a part of me that's missing. And I think you have it..." His voice trailed off.

God damn it! He was making me fall apart—this is not how I wanted to say good-bye. Rivulets of tears streamed down my cheeks.

He tipped up my chin giving me no choice but to meet his passionate gaze. The heat of our breaths filled the air between us. "Gloria, I've never said this to another woman before and if it comes out wrong, I'm going to say it again, again, and again until I get it right. I haven't perfected my pitch. Or even practiced it. My beautiful angel, I l—"

A loud clap of music cut him off. The award ceremony had begun. Strutting onto the stage to loud applause, the gala's emcee, Oprah Winfrey, stunned in a bronze sequined gown. She had readily agreed to host the event because, like me, she was all into girl power and supported underprivileged girls, though hers were in Africa.

While she welcomed the crowd and gave a rundown of tonight's program, Jaime squeezed my hand. I forced myself to focus; my hammering heart was elsewhere, caught between my desperate desire to stay with this magnificent man forever and my desperate need to get away from him as far and as quickly as possible.

In a moving video presentation that Kevin had put together, Oprah narrated the story of Girls Like Us and shared the accomplishments of my philanthropic organization. The beautiful faces of the young girls whose lives I'd helped to change for the better moved me like a tremor in the earth. Through my mentoring program, these underprivileged, neglected, and often abused girls had gone on to become successful professionals and community leaders. Many of them were here in the audience tonight. I felt proud to be among them. There was only one person who I wished could also be here to see me accept my award—Madame Paulette, my own beautiful mentor who had inspired me and changed my life.

The short film was met with loud applause and cheers. Oprah's booming voice quieted the vast room. "And tonight we honor, Gloria Long, CEO of Gloria's Secret, for the amazing work she's done as the founder of Girls Like Us. Please help me bring it on as she comes to the stage to accept her Lifetime Achievement Award."

"Gloria," my signature song, blasted in my ears. My heart leapt into my throat. My big moment had come. But it was not accepting my award that had my nerves crackling with anticipation and apprehension. Immediately afterward, Kevin and I would be making our getaway. My life as I knew it was about to be over. The lyrics of the song resonated with me. Yes, this Gloria was always going to be on the run now too.

Jaime congratulated me again, but before I could thank him, his mouth crashed down on mine in one more fierce, passionate, all-consuming kiss. A deep pang of sadness stabbed at my heart. It was the last time I'd ever feel the touch of his lips on my flesh. On my brain, I immortalized the delicious taste of him, heat of him, and scent of him before pulling away and slowly rising from my chair.

My emotions in total turmoil, I used all my concentration not to stagger up the steps to the stage. With her radiant smile known to millions, Oprah handed me my award —a glimmering gold rose mounted on a plaque. Thanking her, I made my way to the podium. I inhaled a deep breath and took in the sold-out crowd who'd given me a roaring, standing ovation. My heart swelled with joy when I caught sight of the adorable young girls I'd invited jumping up and down. The feeling was fleeting. My teary eyes lingered on only one person—the heartstoppingly beautiful Jaime Zander. He blew me another kiss, and I caught it with my heart. I held his eyes in mine knowing that in just a matter of time I'd never see him again. All I'd have to remember him by were a few tattered petals from his roses that I'd packed last minute.

The crowd took their seats and the applause died down. I gulped another breath of air, thanked everyone, and, then forced myself to wrap my head around my award. *Focus, Gloria.* My mind was in utter chaos, whirling with heart-breaking thoughts of Jaime Zander and my carefully planned escape with Kevin right after my acceptance speech.

I began to wing my speech. My voice was as shaky as my body.

I held up my award. "This golden rose signifies that all girls, regardless of race, looks, or socio-economic background, have the potential to bloom. I was one of those girls, from the wrong side of the tracks, who, thanks to one very special woman, had the chance to turn my life around and suc—"

"Tell them you're a thief!" a familiar voice roared.

"I can prove it with your hair samples. I have the DNA reports!"

The crowd gasped. On the stage was the pink-eyed monster. Boris Borofsky! One hand was clenching the neck of my beloved Kevin and the other was wielding an enormous gun. My heart dropped to my stomach.

"Tell everyone, Gloria, that you stole from me to get to the top, or I'll shoot the brains out of your fag cohort."

"Glorious, don't say anything," begged Kevin, his voice strangled. "He's going to kill us anyway."

"Shut up!" To my horror, Boris fired a random shot into the ballroom. All hell broke loose. Amidst cries for security, panicked attendees clambered over each other to get to the exit doors. Everything was a blur. Where was Jaime? My eyes shifted back to the hostage situation facing me. Pale as a ghost, Kevin didn't flinch or let go of my gaze. I was paralyzed with fear. I knew if I dared make a move, Kevin's life would be over. *Think, Gloria! Think!*

My eyes met Boris's straight on. Maybe I could negotiate with him. "Let go of him," I pleaded. "I paid you back the money. I'll give you more if you want. Name your price."

The hideously scarred Russian snarled at me. Madness flickered in his quartz eyes. "Fuck you, Gloria. Nobody steals from Boris Borofsky."

The words that had haunted me my entire adult life!

I watched helplessly with horror as the mad Russian put his gun to Kevin's jaw. His stumpy forefinger finger curled around the trigger. Kevin's eyes froze wide open. Not a single blink.

"So, pretty boy, how *vould* you like two bullet holes in your cherubic cheeks. Just like the *vuns* you gave me?"

My beloved Kevin was now shaking like a leaf.

The grotesque madman roared with laughter. "Don't *vorry*. I'm going to spare you the pain of having to look every day of your life at the scars left behind. Of people staring at you. Laughing at you. Or of frightened children running away because they think you're a monster!"

Terror filled my racing heart as Boris pulled back the trigger. *CLICK!*

"*Dasvidania, pedik!*"

"Noooooo!" I cried out.

"RUN, Gloria!" Another voice!

Oh my God! Jaime! With the leap of a superhero, he flew through the air and pounced upon Boris and Kevin. Frozen with shock, I couldn't get my feet to move.

"Run, Gloria!" he yelled out again as he wrestled with Boris. Kevin was pinned unconscious under the weight of the Russian's body. The gun, to my horror, went back and forth between the two men.

Sirens blared outside. The battle between Jaime and Boris raged on—with the two men punching, writhing, rolling, banging, cursing, panting—until Boris had the upper hand and the gun. Pinning Jaime to the floor with his stocky brick house body, he pressed the barrel of the gun against Jaime's sweating forehead.

"One move, asshole, and I shoot her first instead," growled Boris.

My beautiful god's denim blue eyes locked onto

mine, filled with desperation and despair. "I love you, Gloria," he mouthed. "Good-bye."

Lustful rage consumed me. I wasn't ready for any good-byes. With an explosive grunt, I hurled my award, the solid golden rose, at Boris. With a loud thud, it struck him in the head. I couldn't believe my luck! Go, girl power! He roared with pain as his gun went flying. While he rubbed the back of his cracked scalp, I raced across the stage and scrambled for the weapon. The madman staggered toward me, blood pouring down his neck. Gripping the heavy weapon with both hands, I aimed it at his heart. I was shaking all over.

"Don't move another step!" My voice quivered. The gun shook in my hand.

"You cunt!" growled the madman taking two steps closer. He was so close I could feel his fetid breath on my cheeks. He reached for the gun. I squeezed it tighter. My torn up finger throbbed.

"Give it back, *suka*. It belongs to me." *Nobody steals from Boris Borofosky.*

"Fuck you, Boris Borofsky!" It was time to end the nightmare. To bury this monster with my secret. I curled my finger around the trigger and pulled it back.

"GLORIA!" yelled Jaime at the top of his lungs.

Boris thrust himself upon me.

At the sound of a deafening explosion, a blinding white light scorched through me. I felt my knees buckle. I hit the floor hard. A rush of pain. And then everything faded to black.

Chapter 13

THE LOUD WAIL OF A siren blared in my eardrums while a sharp pain radiated up my right arm. I fluttered my eyelids, but I couldn't get them to open.

"Gloria."

The soft, velvety, virile voice was familiar. The sound of my name was like a prayer. Comforting, hopeful. I forced my eyes open, one at time. Everything was dark and hazy. Slowly, my pupils focused, and I found myself seated on a bench, cradled in the arms of Jaime Zander. We were moving at lightning speed in some kind of vehicle, the blazing siren still sounding in my ear. Were we on some kind of extreme thrill ride?

Jaime's silky tux jacket was wrapped around my shoulders. Still in my one-shoulder gown, it warmed me. Another sharp pain shot up my arm. I glanced down at my hand. It was swollen and wrapped up in some kind of splint. The bandaged finger that had once worn Jaime's *toi et moi* ring peeked out. It looked puffy and ached. The siren continued to blast as we wove in and out of traffic. It finally dawned on me that I was in the back of an ambulance. Silently, I met Jaime's gaze. Oh, those beautiful denim blues! His eyes held mine with adoration.

"Welcome back, angel." He planted a light kiss on top of my head. "Everything's going to be okay."

Fractured memories of the events that brought me here drifted in my head, creating a dizzying montage. Victor. The FBI taking him down. Vivien falling to pieces. Jaime's passionate kiss. My award. And then the wretched image of a monster invaded my mind. Boris Borofsky! An inner alarm went off. I jerked violently.

"Oh my God. Where's Kevin?"

"I'm over here." My eyes jumped to the rear of the ambulance. Kevin was lying down strapped to a cot, his head propped up on a pillow. With a gasp, I cupped my good hand to my mouth.

"Don't worry, Glorious. I'm fine. The paramedics think I have just a mild concussion, but they want me to go to the hospital to get it checked out."

I smiled with relief. The thought of losing Kevin after all we'd been through was too much to bear.

Kevin lifted his head. "I heard I missed all the action."

Jaime nuzzled my neck. "You were something else, angel. A total tank girl." He started to rebraid my disheveled hair.

"What are you doing, Mr. Zander?"

"What does it look like? I'm braiding your hair. I might as well get used to it since you won't be able to with that cast you'll be getting."

I scrunched my nose. "My arm's broken?"

"Most likely your wrist. A fracture. The next time you shoot someone and decide to faint afterward, please let me know so that I can catch you."

Wait! I shot someone? Another stab of pain rippled through my arm. "Where's Boris?"

"He's dead. You took him out."

My heart should have done a happy dance. I had slain the monster—he was out of my life. Instead, a deluge of tears attacked me. I had no memory of shooting him. The fact that I couldn't remember frightened me.

Jaime brushed away my tears. "Are you okay?"

I nodded. Truthfully, I wasn't sure. My emotions were just one big painful jumble.

"Angel, there's something I want to give back to you." He wrapped his arm around me, his hand skimming my breasts as he dug his fingers into an inside pocket of his jacket. His hand, fisted, re-emerged. Slowly, he unfolded his fingers. Glistening in the middle of his palm was the magnificent *toi et moi* ring.

My heart fluttered at the sight of the two brilliant diamonds—two hearts entwined in an eternal embrace. Tears streamed down my face as I gazed down at my swollen, bandaged finger. "I don't think you'll be able to get it on."

A cocky smile played on his face. "It was never meant for that finger."

What? My breath caught in my throat and my heart hammered madly.

"This, my beautiful angel, is where it belongs."

He lifted my other hand, my left, and slid the ring onto the fourth finger. He then kissed the back of my palm.

I gaped with shock. Hot tears poured down my face. "I don't deserve this. I'm a thief!" I sobbed.

"Yes, a thief of hearts. You stole mine the minute I met you, Gloria." He gently slipped down the one shoulder of my gown dress and placed his warm lips on my scar that was beneath it. The scar that grazed my heart. The scar whose past was now behind me.

I sniffled. "How can I pay you back?"

"There's only way I'm afraid. Give me *your* heart, Gloria. Marry me."

A *toi et moi* forever? My heart was thudding so loud I could hear it. I didn't know what to say.

"Just say yes, Gloria."

Kevin chimed in. "I've already agreed to be best man."

Was this some kind of conspiracy? My eyes ping-ponged from Jaime to Kevin back to Jaime. It didn't get better than this—trapped in an ambulance with the two men I loved the most in the world—differently but equally. I wrapped my good arm around Jaime's neck and smacked my lips into his. The siren that roared in my ear emanated from my heart. Damn it! I loved this man. I needed him like I needed air to breathe.

"Yes," I moaned into his mouth as his arousal pressed against me.

I felt his hand slide down to my breasts; he knew how much I loved it when he massaged them and tweaked my buds. He knew me inside and out. Every inch of me.

Beneath my gown, wetness pooled between my legs and tingles set my core on fire.

Jaime purred into my ear. "I can't wait to devour the future Mrs. Zander every day of my life."

"Don't even think about it, Mr. Zander. You're not getting ambulance sex." Confession: Making love to this incredible man in the back of a speeding ambulance was rather appealing.

"Then let me be the first person to sign your cast," he breathed against my neck.

"What are you going to write?"

Mr. Creativity whispered into my ear. It was astonishingly simple.

JZ♡GL

Toi et moi forever.

Epilogue

Three Months Later

T HE NIGHTMARE OF BEING CHASED by Boris Borofsky is over. I have a new dream. It's always in fifty shades of gray. And it stars Jaime Zander.

"Action! Shoot!"

He carries me down a long winding staircase, shrouded in a cloud of fog. I lie limp, weightless in his bare strong arms, fallen apart from what has been and what will be; the heat of his flesh sears mine. Silk binds my eyes, my hands, and my feet. My breasts, shrouded in cups of leather and lace, quiver with each step he takes. My head is flung back, my platinum hair, loose and long, brushes against his taut torso; my arms dangle. The image of his beautiful face burns through the blindfold and flickers in my head. His hooded eyes are lusting for me, his mouth hungering for every part of me. My core trembles at the thought of what this man can do to me.

Music plays in the background. A song: "Angel" sung by Leona Lewis. The words pipe through my ears. Yes, this was meant to be. He is made for me. I am *his* angel; he is my god. I long for him to devour me with his manliness and make me fall apart until I can scream his name no more.

A seductive, virile voice rises above the music. "Gloria's Secret. Let yourself be carried away."

The dream becomes reality.

"Cut! That's a wrap."

Six Months Later

"Your dress *eez magnifique!*" squees Sandrine, my maid of honor, as she adjusts the long train. It's a body-hugging column of ivory silk and lace, the first in the new line of Gloria's Secret bridal wear we're launching. Beneath it, I have on matching ivory lace lingerie and something borrowed—Sandrine's powder blue garter that she wore at her own fabulous wedding three months ago.

"Gloria, go look at yourself in *zee* mirror," urges my chic French friend with a big smile, looking magnificent herself in an ocean blue satin gown.

I pad over to the floor-length gold-leaf mirror and gaze at myself. My breath hitches. With my waist-length platinum hair flowing over my shoulders, the way my future husband adores it, and my angelic makeup, I almost don't recognize myself. The brilliant red lipstick on my lips reminds me of who I am. The sexy, powerful CEO of Gloria's Secret, and the future wife of Mr. Jaime Zander.

The dress is strapless. I wear my pearl-white scar on my chest like jewelry. I no longer have to hide it. Scars come with secrets and mine has been bared. It reminds me that I have survived. That I have healed. I have left my past behind.

While I stare at my reflection, Sandrine carefully places the final piece of my ensemble over my head—Madame Paulette's delicate Chantilly lace veil that she wore when she married her beloved Henri. Along with many other things that I'll always cherish, she left it to me in her will. I adjust it so that it obscures my face.

"Ah, *ma chérie*, you look *superbe!*" That deep raspy voice. It's Madame Paulette! I can hear her. She's here!

"*Merci, Madame,*" I say silently. I smile at my reflection, and it smiles back at me.

"Holy fuck! Glorious, you look beyond fabulous!"

I pivot on my red-soled ivory satin Louboutins. Yes, a touch of red from head to toe.

It's Kevin. My best friend and best man. He's gone English morning suit the whole way—well, except for the red Keds. That's what makes my beloved Kevin who he is.

Jogging up to me, he gives me a great big hug.

"I just had to take a peek," he gushes. "Gotta go and check on Ray." He rolls his eyes. "That boy is so high maintenance and takes forever to get ready."

I stifle a laugh. Jaime's assistant, Ray, followed him to LA and, after breaking up with his New York boyfriend, hooked up again with Kevin. They're living together in Kevin's condo one floor below mine. Happiness soars in my heart knowing how happy and in love my Kev is. An over-the-top Christmas wedding is in the works, and to my sheer delight, Kevin is marrying into a wonderful family that embraces his homosexuality. I give him a peck on the cheek before he scurries out of my bedroom.

Tyrone is waiting for me downstairs. Jaime and I are exchanging our vows on the beach below the cliff where we plan to build our dream house. Everyone from his company and mine has been invited; no gifts permitted except donations to Girls Like Us, my charitable mentoring program. I hope all the underprivileged girls I support will find as much meaning and joy as I have in my life.

Only two prominent Gloria's Secret associates—or should I say former associates—won't be there. Victor Holden and his daughter Vivien. Victor is no longer affiliated with Gloria's Secret. In fact, he's no longer affiliated with any of his companies. Soon after his arrest, he was indicted by a grand jury and later found guilty on three counts of securities fraud. Further investigation into his dealings had proven that he'd also funded Boris Borofsky's sex slave trade. He was charged a hefty fine and sentenced to three years in a white-collar penitentiary without parole. After her father was sentenced, Vivien fled the country. Sandrine thinks she saw her in Greece while on her honeymoon; that's one place Jaime and I won't be visiting soon.

Jaime's ad campaign in which we starred was a great success and has even been nominated for several awards. Sales have soared. The subsequent sex toy launch was also phenomenal. Just as Jaime had proven in his little one-on-one research session, women—and couples—love the provocative products. They've sold like hotcakes, and Gloria's Secret stock has gone through the roof. It's at an all-time high.

We're still looking for a new Chairman of the

Board. One of the Board members suggested Jaime, but he declined, stating it was a conflict of interest. Besides, he's too busy running his own company ZAP! whose headquarters he moved to California. It made sense. He has a lot of clients in Los Angeles and Silicon Valley as well as in Japan, China, and other Asian countries. And he has all of me. His new office, overlooking the ocean in Santa Monica, is a fifteen-minute drive from mine. Needless to say, we do lunch. Or we'll squeeze in a quick work out together. My inner thighs have never been in better shape.

The SoCal late summer day cannot be more perfect. It's the kind of weather that makes people flock to LA and never want to leave —a cloudless blue sky, a perfect mild temperature, and just a little ocean breeze. Going on six in the evening, the fiery sun is beginning its descent into the ocean. The sound of the ocean with its crashing waves mixes with squawking gulls. That is the only music Jaime and I wanted when we exchanged our vows.

My heart is pounding with anticipation as I walk down the cliffside steps, that Jaime had built just in time for our wedding, on the arms of two other men dear to my heart—my drivers, Tyrone and Nigel. The latter flew in on the corporate jet from New York to be here for me. The memory of Jaime chasing after his town car after I fled from him flickers in my head. I hold back a bittersweet tear. I'm so lucky he never stopped chasing me. In my right hand, I hold two fragrant long stemmed roses—one white for Madame Paulette, the other red for Jaime. The two people who have made me blossom as a woman.

My heart skips a beat when I see my man. Oh God, he's gorgeous, dressed in an elegant long-tailed tux and a blue bow tie that complements the color of his eyes. And of course, no socks. His denim blues meet my gaze and I know he's mine. Later tonight, we're flying back to Paris on his private plane for our honeymoon. The City of Light. And the City of Love. I glimpse down at my shimmering *toi et moi* ring and wonder what surprises Mr. Creativity has in store for me this time.

"Come here, you." He takes me in his arms. I melt.

"You look beautiful, Gloria," he whispers in my ear. Oh, the breathy way he says my name!

"You do too," I whisper back.

Before a justice of the peace and an adoring crowd of coworkers, we exchange our vows. My heart hammers as Jaime begins.

"My angel, I showed you my scars; you showed me yours. I gave you my heart and you gave me yours. We are the eternal union of two wounded souls. But from this day on, no more scars; no more pain. I will love you, cherish you, and protect you for all of eternity."

It's my turn. I'm teary-eyed.

"*Mon amour*, I promise I will love you forever. No matter what life throws at us, we will always be *toi et moi*. I shall never leave you. My tears are my witness. And I shall keep no secrets between us for as long as we both shall live."

We exchange simple gold bands, mine inscribed with the word *"toi"* and his with *"moi."* We're officially husband and wife. My heart roars with joy as Jaime lifts up my veil, and his lush lips consume mine with a passionate kiss that I want never to end.

This is the man I will cherish and confide in the rest of my life. He knows all my secrets. I bore my past—my abusive childhood with my crack whore mother, my love for Madame Paulette, and the unthinkable crime that's now behind me, buried six feet under. One night after making glorious love, I even confessed to initially thinking he was Ms. Zander. A woman! He almost rolled off the bed with laughter and then fucked me again...harder.

Confession: There's one more secret. I'm hiding it deep inside me. But true to my vow, Jaime was the first to know. In six months, the world will know too.

Her name is Paulette Long Zander. And she has a twin. We're calling him Payton Henri.

THE END

Bonus:

The First Chapter Of Gloria's
Secret From Jaime's Pov

When Jaime Met Gloria

"**H**OLD THE DOOR," I YELLED out as I jogged to the elevator. Damn it! I didn't want to miss it. Lately, the elevator had been acting up. If I didn't make it, I might have to wait ten minutes for another car. Maybe more. I'd meant to report the problem to maintenance, but hadn't had the chance. Living in a full-service hotel came with its perks, but owning it came with its headaches.

When I got to the elevator, the doors were parted about a foot. I could hear someone inside it frantically pounding at the panel of floor buttons. Whoever it was, he or she was hitting the wrong button—not the "Open Door" button. People in a panic often did that.

With the doors now just a palm's width apart, I had no choice. I slid my hand between them, cursing under my breath that they wouldn't close and crush it. Luck! The doors slid back open. I blew out a sigh of relief.

When I stepped into the car, there was indeed a passenger inside. A blond, well-dressed woman, who was squatting, collecting photos that were scattered around her and stuffing them back into her leather briefcase—Chanel for sure.

"Let me help you," I said, already bending down to come to her aid.

Her gaze met mine. I recognized her immediately. Gloria Long, the thirty-three-year-old CEO and founder of Gloria's Secret, the world's largest chain of lingerie stores. Since I was meeting her shortly to discuss the possibility of handling her advertising, I'd googled her.

While she was stunning online, she was even more beautiful in person. Her face was heart-shaped with porcelain skin and lush lips so red they needed no lipstick—though they'd look hot in a warm shade of scarlet. Her hair was rare platinum, and she wore it in a tight braid—the rope so long it skimmed the polished floor. Yet, there was something different about her up close and personal. It took me a moment to figure it out. Online, her wide-set eyes appeared to be chocolate, but face-to-face, one eye was dark topaz and the other sapphire. I'd read about her weird idiosyncrasy somewhere, but couldn't remember its name. Several celebrities shared it, including Mila Kunis and Kate Bosworth. It made Ms. Long intriguing and even sexier.

While I recognized her, she didn't appear to recognize me—Jaime Zander, the founder and CCO of ZAP! After some thought, I decided not to reveal my identity. I was looking forward to her reaction when she met with me shortly. Was she in for a surprise! I loved playing games.

"Interesting photos." My eyes lingered on one particularly sexy one of a D-cupped model fondling her breasts. I picked it up gingerly with my fingers. "Hmm... I think I fucked her once." I picked up another. "She looks familiar too."

"Give me those." She snatched the photos from

my hand and hastily stuffed them into her briefcase with the others.

Let the games begin. "Are you a photographer?"

She sneered. "Hardly."

"So, you're some kind of pervert who collects photos of semi-naked girls with big tits."

"And you're some kind of pervert who likes to sleep with them."

Her comeback was quick. So, she was a sassy one. I liked that about her.

She shot me a dirty look and continued to collect the photos. We both reached for the last one at once. My fingers met her perfectly manicured fingertips. They were burning. A heat wave coursed through me. Leaving my hand next to hers longer than needed, I let her file it away.

After zipping up her briefcase, she realized that the elevator doors were still open, and we weren't moving. Neither of us had remembered to hit the "close" button. Rising to my feet, I did the favors. Her gaze rode up my long, muscular legs. She was definitely checking me out. I felt my cock straining against my jeans. She was having an effect on me.

The elevator descended, but before she could get to her feet, it came to a jolting halt. Damn this elevator. Mental note: Talk to maintenance and get them on the case. I glanced down at my companion. All color had drained from her lovely face, and she bit down on her sensuous lips.

"Are you okay?" I asked, crouching down again.

She nodded nervously. I resisted the urge to hold her pale face in my hands but couldn't help brushing the silky tip of her braid across her strong chin. I told her that this happened all the time with this elevator.

Without warning, the elevator jerked again and began to free fall. Ms. Long gasped. I longed to hold her securely in my arms and tell her to not be afraid. Instead, I simply reminded her that this was an express elevator; there was nothing to worry about.

We reached the lobby in no time. A ping sounded and the doors opened wide. Ms. Long let me help her to her feet. It couldn't be easy getting up in her tight pencil skirt and six-inch heels. She straightened her stoic black suit, Chanel again, without a thank-you.

Standing face-to-face, I drank in her entire body in full view for the first time. Considering that I stood six foot three, she must have been about five foot seven minus her stilettos. Her legs were long and shapely, the kind that seemed endless. And beneath her suit jacket strained a fine set of tits. Definitely a C-cup. Maybe even a D. She was as beautiful and sexy as any Gloria's Secret model. Yeah, she was fuckable, but why was she so uptight?

She fired me another dirty look and shot out of the elevator. Her gait was strong and confident, as if she'd been born wearing heels. My eyes settled on her ass as I trailed close behind her. What an ass! I couldn't get over the way it moved in smooth figure eights. Damn! This woman gave off mixed messages.

Her pace was fast, but I had no trouble keeping up with her. She kept her head up high and her spine straight, completely ignoring me.

Outside the tall steel and glass building, we stood side by side. The morning rush of cabs and limos crowded the circular driveway. My car, the third in line, would be pulling up to the curb soon.

"Can I give you a ride?" I asked. "My driver will be here any minute." *And we're headed to the same destination.*

"Thanks but no thanks," she retorted, her voice icy. "I have my own driver."

"Impressive."

She didn't miss my sarcasm and shot me a smirk. Fuck. She was sexy when she did that little curl of her lips.

My car, a sleek black Ranger Rover, pulled up first. One of the valets raced to open the passenger door.

"See ya." I winked as sidled into the car. She gave me one final dirty look. After the valet slammed the door shut and we pulled away, I laughed my head off. She was going to see me in less than an hour. I couldn't wait.

My agency, ZAP!, which stood for Zander and People, was located in the heart of Soho on Prince Street. I smiled, as I always did, when Orson, my driver dropped me in front of the late nineteenth century brick townhouse.

Our receptionist, Brandy, was putting on her headset when I breezed into my office headquarters. She was clad in a graphic tee with a portrait of Jim Morrison printed on it, and on her arm, I swore she sported a brand new tattoo. Before long, her arm would be sleeved with tattoos. Her eyes fluttered at the sight of me. I couldn't deny the effect I had on women—even on husky-voiced biker chicks like her.

"Good morning, Jaime."

Everyone at the office was on a first-name basis, and the atmosphere was casual. No stuffy suits here. Even I wore jeans to the office most of the time.

"Hi, Brandy," I winked at her as I skirted past her desk and loped down the gutted corridor to my office. I was pleased to pass so many employees already at work. Most of them were young and passionate—I liked having talented, recent grads around me.

My assistant, Ray, was already at his desk when I got there. It didn't matter that he was blatantly gay. A RISD graduate, he was brilliant and my protégé. He had a big career as an art director ahead of him.

"The SIN-TV team is in the screening room waiting for you to view the spot they just cut."

SIN-TV was a recently launched porn network based in Los Angeles that had hired us to create a brand identity and a national advertising campaign. The tagline we'd come up with, "Television so hot, your screen will sizzle," had blown away CEO, Blake Burns, and we'd subsequently become good buddies.

"Great. Let me just check my e-mails and I'll head over there."

I flew into my office, threw my leather bomber jacket onto a cool-looking coat rack, and made a beeline for my desk.

I loved my desk. It was a large, light-wood elliptical table that I'd found at a local antiques shop. I kept little on it—my state-of-the-art computer, a few colorful plastic folders, and a framed photo of my father and me at the beach taken at the age of five. I stared at the photo and could still remember the day it was taken as if it were yesterday. Our favorite secret spot in Malibu where he liked to paint. The memory brought me as much sadness as joy. A day didn't go by without missing him.

I booted up my computer and went directly to my e-mail inbox. Most of the new e-mails could wait, but one caught my attention and made my entire body tense up. It was from Vivien Holden and it said URGENT in the subject line. What the fuck did she want? With hesitation, I clicked it open.

Hi, Jaime!

I'm here. Why don't you come to the Gloria's Secret Fashion Show at the Lexington Avenue Armory? I've reserved a ticket in your name.

Mwah! Vivien

The last person I wanted to see was Vivien Holden, Gloria Long's assistant. Make that the next to last person. Her scumbag father, Victor, the Chairman of Gloria's Secret, was tops on my list. Gloria had no idea that I personally knew them both. And I planned to keep it that way for as long as possible.

I didn't reply and stormed out of my office. Passing by Ray's desk again, I told him to let me know when my ten o'clock meeting—Gloria Long—arrived. Just saying her name made my cock twitch. I couldn't wait to see the expression on her face when she saw me.

The rough cut for the SIN-TV spot looked great. With the right music and graphics, it was going to rock. Blake would be happy. After giving a few notes to my creative team, the screening room phone rang.

I picked it up myself. It was Ray, informing me that Ms. Long had arrived.

I dashed out of the screening room and sprinted back to my office. She was seated on one of my Scandinavian arms chairs, scrolling e-mails on her iPhone. One long leg was crossed over the other. Upon hearing my footsteps, her head pivoted to the doorway. Her jaw dropped and her phone slipped out of her hand. Oh, she was shocked all right. She couldn't get her mouth to close as I strode up to her. She hesitantly stood up, and I shook her hand. What I thought would be warm and soft was wet and clammy. I had her good!

"Gloria, a pleasure to meet you officially." It took all I had to stifle laughter.

She still couldn't get her mouth to move. Finally, she said, "And you're..."

"Jaime Zander."

She froze. I almost felt sorry for her as she collapsed back into the chair. I took the chair catty-cornered to hers. I was so close to her that I could hear her heart thudding.

"Are you sure I can't get you something? A coffee? Water? Tea perhaps?" *Prozac?*

"No, thank you," she stammered and tugged nervously at her long braid.

I had the burning urge to undo her rope of platinum and run my fingers through her lustrous hair as it cascaded over shoulders and down her back. In my mind's eye, I could picture what she'd look like with her wavy hair loose. A goddess.

She cleared her throat and met my eyes. "As you know, Mr. Zander, I'm looking for an advertising agency to help me expand my business. I want to take Gloria's Secret to a new level of sales and sensuality."

Without losing eye contact, I leaned back into my chair. "Gloria's Secret. The #1 lingerie chain in the world. 2045 stores worldwide. Estimated annual sales revenue: 3.5 billion dollars."

Oh, she was impressed for sure. But Ms. Poker Face simply gave a little nod and told me that she needed to stay ahead of the competition. And then her brows knitted together.

"Did you read *Fifty Shades of Grey?*" Her tone was challenging.

"Are you testing me, Gloria?"

"It's Ms. Long and yes, I am...Well?"

Ha! She was in for another surprise. I'd actually read it way before it'd become a phenomenon. One of my hook-ups had left behind the paperbacks at my hotel suite. It was quite amusing though Mr. Grey could have learned a thing or two from me.

Without wasting a second, I replied, "Grace Trevelyn Grey. And she's a pediatrician."

Her brows furrowed again. *Score another one for me.*

"Mr. Zander—"

"Please call me Jaime."

"Okay, then, *Jai-me,* tell me, what, in your opinion, has made the book so popular with women?"

I gazed into her mesmerizing two-color eyes. "Truthfully, while the sex is hot, I believe women fall for the romance."

Her eyes narrowed. "What do you mean?"

"Well, Ms. Long, wouldn't you like me to scoop

you up in arms...tell you that 'I want you, body and soul, forever'...and make insane love to you on the couch?"

She flushed a lovely shade of pink. Ooh, I really got to her that time—Mr. Grey at his best. Her eyes jumped back and forth between my crotch and the couch. She looked all heated up...maybe I should offer her a glass of water again. Nah. Let's keep it going.

I leaned into her and growled into her ear. "Or would you prefer me to throw you over my desk... or perhaps carry you away and devour you on the conference room table down the hall?"

She squirmed and nervously started swinging one of her shapely crossed legs. I was enjoying every minute. The truth is, I was actually fantasizing tearing off that uptight suit and fucking her anywhere I could. My cock was straining against my jeans.

She must have been reading my mind. Seen through my eye fuck. She jerked back and deliberately kept her eyes away from the area between my inner thighs.

She took a deep breath. "You seem to know women quite well."

I sat back in my chair. "Yes, I do." *You have no idea.*

"In my experience, the only men who understand women are gay. Are you by chance, gay, Jaime?"

She thought I was gay? Was she being serious or funny? I refrained from bursting into laughter. "Hardly. I could have several hundred stunning women give you a stellar recommendation." *Or was it several thousand? I'd lost count.*

To my shock, my statement failed to get a rise out of her. "Oh, so you have them review you like you're a book on Amazon?"

This time I laughed aloud; she was a regular stand-up comic. "You're rather quite witty, Ms. Long. I like that in a woman."

The truth, I'd never met any woman quite like her. She was feisty, independent, and strong-willed. And she wasn't falling all over me. She was in a word: a challenge.

I moved in closer to her and snagged her braid, coiling it around my long fingers. It was almost like some kind of bondage accessory.

I breathed against her willowy neck. "So, Ms. Long, what will it take to win your account?" *And your cunt?*

Ms. Feisty promptly removed my hand and looked me straight in the eyes. "I've asked every agency I've met with to come up with a pitch by Friday. Do you think your agency could do that?"

I assured her we could. "I'll put my best person on the job."

Her eyebrows arched. "And who might that be?"

I shot her a wicked grin. "Yours truly," I said as I rose and escorted her to the door. But she was not leaving yet. I barricaded the door with my body, stretching my muscular arms across the frame. Face- to-face, I could feel her sweet breath warm my cheeks. Her eyes met mine in a heated exchange.

"I meant to tell you, Ms. Long, I find your eyes fascinating."

Though I'm sure most people did, they widened as if she were a little surprised.

"They're contradictions just like the rest of you."

Now, her eyes grew really round. "What do you mean?"

"Your mind says one thing; your body says another."

She twitched; I was on to her. "Mr. Zander, can I please leave?"

With a triumphant smirk, I let her pass but not before tugging at her braid. "Ms. Long, I look forward to the *pleasure* of seeing you again."

"The same," she hissed.

I wanted badly to win her account even if she was going to be one damn tough client. My eyes stay riveted on her as she stomped down the hallway. Fuck, those long legs! That perfectly rounded ass! I swear, I could see right through her layers of clothing.

"Oh, by the way, I find the black lace push-up bra you're wearing and the matching thong very sexy. And that garter..." My voice trailed off.

Without looking back at me, she kept moving and, in fact, quickened her pace, tightening her grip around her briefcase handle. I didn't have to see her face to know that it was all screwed up. That scrunchy thing she did turned me on. A hard-on was raging beneath my jeans. Yes, I was determined to win a lot more than her account. Whatever it took, I was going to win her.

Playlist

Here are some of the songs that inspired *Gloria's Secret* and *Gloria's Revenge;* many of them are featured within the books. The hit songs of the late, great Laura Branigan were a major source of inspiration, especially "Gloria," whose lyrics fit so well with Gloria's story. If you are not familiar with this amazing artist, I hope you will take the time to get to know her.

"Gloria"/Laura Branigan
"Self Control"/Laura Branigan
"Take a Bow"/Rihanna
"Blurred Lines"/Robin Thicke
"La Vie en Rose"/Edith Piaf
"Undercover Lover"/Kids in Glass Houses
"Toi et Moi"/Charles Aznavour
"Je ne Regrette Rien"/Edith Piaf
"Crazy"/Gnarls Barkley
"Good Vibrations"/The Beach Boys
"Bleeding Love"/Leona Lewis
"Jar of Hearts"/Christina Perri
"Just Give me a Reason"/Pink
"Nobody Ever Told You"/Carrie Underwood
"How Am I Supposed to Live Without You"/Laura Branigan
"Angel"/Leona Lewis

Acknowledgments

Another big shout out to Team Gloria...

My beta readers in alphabetical order...Michele Coddington, Adriane Leigh, Cindy Meyers, and Jen Oreto. You were all beyond fabulous with your insightful comments and suggestions.

My *chère amie,* Arianne Richmonde, author of the bestselling *Pearl* series, who cheered me on and offered to find those last minute typos. *Je t'adore!*

The passionate bloggers who have stood by me through thick and thin.

My you-know-who-you-are-dear Facebook and Twitter fans whose kind words got me through the final chapters and the long, difficult edit ahead.

My cover artist and formatter, Glendon Haddix of Streetlight Graphics.

My proofreader, Kathie Middlemiss of Kat's Eye Editing.

My family. Thank you for putting up with me while I'm glued to my computer and can't always be the mommy you need and want.

Last but not least, I also want to express my gratitude to all my readers. I hope you enjoyed *Gloria's Secret* and *Gloria's Revenge* and will take the time to leave reviews. To writers like me, even a short review means so much and helps others discover my books.

Thank you. Love you all.
MWAH!~Nelle

About the Author

Nelle L'Amour is a *New York Times* and *USA Today* bestselling author who lives in Los Angeles with her Prince Charming-ish husband, twin teenage princesses, and a bevy of royal pain-in-the-butt pets. A former executive in the entertainment and toy industries with a prestigious Humanitas Award behind her, she gave up playing with Barbies a long time ago, but still enjoys playing with toys...with her husband. While she writes in her PJ's, she loves to get dressed up and pretend she's Hollywood royalty. She aspires to write juicy stories with characters that will make you both laugh and cry and stay in your heart forever.

She is also the bestselling author of the critically acclaimed erotic love story, *Undying Love*, and the erotic romance series, *Seduced by the Park Avenue Billionaire*. Additionally, she is featured in the bestselling romance anthology, *Billionaire Bad Boys of Romance*. Writing under another pen name, she is the author of the highly rated fantasy/romance: *Dewitched: The Untold Story of the Evil* Queen, an Amazon Top 100 bestseller, and its sequel, *Unhitched*.

Nelle is currently working on her next novels, *That Man*, which features more of Jaime and Gloria, and *Endless Love*, the sequel to *Undying Love*.

Nelle loves to hear from her readers. Please "like" her author Facebook page and write to her at the email address below so that she can include you in her mailing list and keep you updated with any new publications.

nellelamour@gmail.com
www.facebook.com/NelleLamourAuthor
www.twitter.com/nellelamour

Seduced by the Park Avenue Billionaire

By Nelle L'amour

1

I 'M GOING TO MISS MY train! That was all I could
think of as I dashed through the stately entrance to
Philadelphia's majestic 30th Street Station. My best
friend Lauren, with all her connections, had scored
a bunch of coveted tickets to the Black Eyed Peas
concert in Central Park, and I was among those she
had chosen to be among her entourage... so I had to
be home by seven, shower, and get dressed. I rushed
past the tempting food court toward the information
center. The old-fashioned flip-letter Amtrak Train
information board made a ticking sound as it
updated arrivals and departures. I glanced up. Shit!
My train to Penn Station was leaving in five minutes
from Gate 5. My eyes darted around the elegant art-
deco station for the escalator leading down to the
train platform. Despite how many times I had been
in this vast station over the past several months, I
never knew where I was going. My sense of direction
was nothing to be proud of.

My eyes bounced from the famous Angel of the
Resurrection statue to another bronzed statue. A
god. A 6'2" golden-haired Adonis perched on the VIP
mezzanine. Even from this distant vantage point,
I could I could tell he was wearing one of those

super-expensive custom- tailored beige suits that New York's tycoons donned once Spring hit. It made a stunning contrast with his St. Tropez tan, the kind wealthy Manhattanites sported all year round. With his expensive designer glasses perched on his perfectly blown flaxen hair, he looked like he was right out of *GQ.*

I couldn't get my eyes off him. The sight of him made my knees weak and my heart hammer. I had dreamt of men like this, but they were way out of my league. The chance of ever meeting one was unlikely. Make that never. I was a geeky, recent college who, after several false starts, had finally landed an entry-level job at Ike's Tikes, an established New York City toy company, and was struggling to make ends meet. Beautiful men were just not in my cards. They never had been. But my mom had always told me it was okay to dream. And for a minute, as Adonis pivoted his head in my direction, I imagined his eyes burning across the station into mine.

A booming voice put an end to my reverie—and the pulsating I felt between my legs. "Last call for Amtrak 148 to Penn Station boarding at Gate 5." In a blink of an eye, Adonis was gone. Out of my life and dreams forever. My heart rate accelerated as my eyes flickered around the expansive station for the gate sign. Finally, I found it and began to run, my messenger-style leather bag flying behind me. The escalator descending to the train platform was out of order. Thank goodness, I was wearing my trusty combat boots. At breakneck speed, I clambered down the daunting three flights of stairs, praying that the train wouldn't leave without me.

"Wait!" I screamed as the automatic doors of the sleek silver train were closing. I skimmed through one of them, narrowly missing being a smooshed sardine.

Breathing heavy, I staggered through the car, desperately searching for a seat. Nothing. It was rush hour and every seat was taken. Maybe I would have better luck in the next car, I thought as I wobbled across the connecting bridge, the train rolling into motion. I so needed to sit down, catch my breath, and relax. I was exhausted and rundown. Not just from my sprint to the train, but from months of juggling my Manhattan-based job as the assistant to a demanding female executive with visits to my ailing mother who was receiving experimental cancer treatments at the world-renowned Hospital of the University of Pennsylvania. Seeing my mother in her weakened state, hooked up to IV's and machines, never helped no matter how cheery she was when I came to see her.

As the train picked up speed, I struggled to keep my balance and open the sliding door to the next car. Using all the muscle power I could, I finally yanked it open and tumbled into the cabin. This car was different than the one before. It was far more spacious and deluxe. Roomy pairs of rich brown leather seats lined the aisles, and the well-dressed occupants were sipping cocktails in real glasses and toying with the latest electronic gadgets. This was obviously business-class. I sure as hell did not belong here wearing my T.J. Maxx midi skirt and Fruit of the Loom t-shirt. Oh yeah, and my worn out combat boots, a treasured gift from my mom. This was the cabin where Louis Vuittons, Jimmy Choos, and Chanels mingled with other LVs, Jimmies, and Cocos. No, I didn't belong here. Not one bit.

Fighting the speed of the train and my embarrassment, I clumsily zigzagged down the aisle, occasionally grabbing onto the corner of a seat for balance. Like the previous cabin, every seat was taken. No one seemed to notice me, but truthfully, I wanted to get out of here as quickly as possible. As I neared the rear end of the car, the train jerked, sending me flying into the lap of a *Wall Street Journal*-reading commuter to my left.

"I'm so sorry," I squeaked at my victim whose face was still buried in his *WSJ*.

He flexed his leg muscles under my muscular butt, signaling me to get up, and then slowly lowered his newspaper. A smirk curled on his lips. *Oh those lips!*

My heart leaped into my throat. Adonis!

"Sit," he said, motioning to the empty window seat next to his.

"Um, uh, I'm in economy," I stuttered, my eyes unable to leave his face no matter how humiliated I felt. Up close, he was even more beautiful than I imagined with his chiseled nose, strong angular jaw line, and piercing eyes, the color of sapphires.

"Don't worry; I'll handle it," he said with a wink.

Holy shit! Adonis had just winked at me!

"Sit," he growled, this time as if it were an order.

With a powerful heave of his knees, he bounced me to my feet, forcing me to plop down next to him.

Holy shit again! I was going to spend the next hour and a half sitting next to this gorgeous man—a man that existed only in my dreams—and now I had no idea what to say. My heart pounded.

"What's your name?" he asked, in a coy tone that suggested he was daring me to answer.

"Sarah," I replied, pulling myself together in time to reply in a very business-like voice.

"Saarah," he repeated, his voice deep and sexy.

The way he said my name drawing out the first syllable with breathiness—sent a chill down my spine. I could not help thinking of lyrics from my all-time favorite movie, *West Side Story*. "Say it soft and it's almost like praying."

"Ari," he said next, not giving me time to ask the obvious.

A fitting name. Almost like Ares, the Greek god of war. This man was a warrior. A beautiful warrior. And I was soon to find out that conquest was his middle name.

I held out my slender hand to shake his. Truthfully, I didn't know what else to do. His long, tan fingers entwined mine. His grip was strong. Powerful. Slowly, he raised my hand to his lush lips. Blood rushed to my head as they pressed ever so gently against the back of my palm. One by one, he unfolded my fingers, sucking each one as if they were candy sticks. The wetness of his warm saliva glistened on my fingertips. Butterflies fluttered in my stomach, and moisture pooled between my legs. *What the hell was he doing? And why the hell was I letting him do it?*

My heart was racing as fast as the Amtrak. I needed to stop this. Move to another seat. My eyes darted around the cabin, but there were still none to be had. No one seemed to notice what was going on; they either had their faces buried in newspapers or books or were occupied with their smartphones, iPads, or eReaders.

This was just not right. I was sitting next to a complete stranger and letting him suck my fingers. He could be a total whack job... a molester... or serial killer. Who knew? Though my fear was fleeting, I made up a desperate clichéd excuse. "Um, uh excuse me. I need to use the restroom." Actually, I really did. I needed to get away from this mysterious, seductive stranger and get a grip.

"It's right behind us," said Adonis dryly, returning to his newspaper.

I leaped up from my seat. Tripping over my bag, I caught a glimpse of Trainman's bemused expression. He refused to move his long legs, forcing my butt to brush against them as I made my escape.

The door to the unisex restroom located at the back of the cabin was locked. That meant someone was inside. I tapped my foot impatiently, my head filling with the image of the blond, blue-eyed Adonis sitting next to me. Why couldn't I stop thinking about him? These kinds of things never happened to geeky me. They were the stuff of novels and movies. Not my boring all-work-no-play life.

"Hi." A familiar velvety voice catapulted me out of my thoughts, and a waft of warm breath blew across the nape of my neck. I spun around.

My mysterious stranger. His crisp blue eyes burned into mine, making my temperature soar and my legs turn to jelly. What was he doing here? I suppose he had to go. I couldn't stop that.

I turned my head away and stared squarely at the bathroom door, praying silently that whoever was in there would hurry up. He blew hot air on my neck again and wrapped his arms around my waist, pulling me tight against his rock-hard body. A bulge pressed against my buttocks. I was getting sick to my stomach and might need the bathroom more than I'd originally thought.

Finally, the door burst open in my face; a sour-faced, overweight matron barged out. Calling on every muscle in my body, I broke free of Trainman's grip and hastily dashed into the stall and the stench she left behind. My hands shaky, I fumbled to slide the latch, but before I could get it through the lock, the door forcefully swung open.

"I couldn't wait," Trainman growled, pushing me against the cold metal sink basin. He thrust his hips tight against mine. I was trapped.

He leaned in close to me. A mix of his warm minty breath and expensive cologne rushed into my nostrils, eradicating all traces of the fetid odor. His eyes narrowed, turning into collectible slivers of blue sand glass. His mouth descended onto the right side of my neck then slowly trailed upward to my earlobe. He clamped his warm, moist lips on the cartilage, alternating between nipping and sucking it. Oh my God! I didn't know my earlobes could feel so much. The last time they felt anything was when I got them pierced in eighth grade. And that was pain. Pure pain. Now what I was feeling was joy. Pure tingly joy... and the sensation was coursing through my entire body.

Still pressing me hard against the sink with his

hipbones, he pinched my dime-size nipples between his thumb and index fingers and then began massaging them in small counterclockwise circles, each rotation harder than the one before. Magically, the buds elongated and hardened beneath my cotton t-shirt. A new I-want-to-burst-out-of-my skin sensation gathered in the triangle between my legs. I moaned softly.

"You don't wear a bra," he murmured in my ear.

I rarely wore a bra because I really didn't need one. My boobs never got past a small A-cup, the size of old-fashioned champagne saucers. Before I could say a word, that is if I could utter a word, he whispered, "Sexy."

Moi, Sarah plain and tall, sexy? And this coming from this gorgeous beast? Pinch me. I must be dreaming this entire fantasy. As if on cue, he pinched one of my nipples again. My crotch roared silently in delight. No, this was real okay. And it was happening to me. Sarah Greene. Art school graduate. Aspiring toy designer. Twenty-five-year-old virgin.

I stared at his beautiful face. His eyes were tilted downward. A sly smile tipped to the left made me nervous. In a good way.

While one hand continued to twirl a nipple, the other slid down my torso past by tight, twisted abdomen and under the elastic waistbands of both my skirt and pantyhose. His hands felt like hot velvet as they explored my inner thighs.

"Hmm," he moaned. "No panties?"

I never wore panties with pantyhose. Why bother? They were called pantyhose for a reason.

And I confess, not buying expensive panties—and bras—saved me a lot of money—money I needed desperately to visit my sick mother.

"Very sexy," he said, enunciating each syllable, as his fingertips made their way to the triangle between my legs. They stopped to caress my patch of hair, stroking it as if were a beloved pussy... cat.

"So soft and silky," Trainman purred as if I were auditioning for one of those look-at-my-gorgeous-hair shampoo commercials.

After a tug of a curled clump, his fingers moved to the smooth folds between my legs. He explored this new territory eagerly like someone who was searching for gold. And then he discovered it. The nugget. Greedily, he rubbed the pad of this thumb around his discovery with intense little circles that were driving me insane. A loud moan escaped my lips.

"You're so wet," he crooned.

That was an understatement. I was swimming in my own juices. My eyes caught a glimpse of him. A wicked smile crossed his face, and his blue eyes glistened.

He squeezed the folds of my labia together and then used his fingers to spread them apart.

"I want you," he moaned, his voice all hot and breathy.

And despite myself, I wanted him. More than anyone or anything. Well, except for my mother getting well again.

Still massaging my nub with his thumb, he plunged his long middle finger into the cavity between the folds. I gasped, not prepared for the shock of penetration. Shockwaves spread throughout my body as his finger glided up and down the soaked, spongy walls. In and out, each thrust deeper than the one before.

"Baby," he moaned. "You're so hot."

I sucked in air between my teeth, still not sure this was really happening. My core was aching for more. Desperate for it. Why was I not resisting?

"I'm going to take you now," he growled.

Take me where? I didn't want to be anywhere, any place but here in this cramped bathroom with this mysterious sorcerer who was doing his magic on me.

Using his free hand, he yanked down both my skirt and hose. My eyes glanced down at my skirt puddled on the floor and my pantyhose scrunched up above my combat boots. As they made their way back upward, I heard him unzip his fly. My gaze stopped short at a massive hunk of pink, veined flesh that was aimed at my crotch. *Yowzer!* I was ready to surrender. Yes, take me now.

"Sit on the sink," he ordered.

I was in no condition to argue. I plunked my buttocks down on the edge of the steely basin. The cold metal gave me goose bumps all over. He pulled off my boots and the hose. "Now, spread your legs."

Yes, sir.

He placed both hands on my boyishly narrow hips to anchor me. An intensity washed over his face. Like an artist who was contemplating painting his masterpiece.

"Now, take me and insert me where you want me."

Holy shit! He wanted me to touch that monstrosity? Cradle it in my hands? Our eyes met, mine wide-eyed with fear and excitement, his hooded with determination and desire.

Hesitantly, I wrapped my slender fingers around the pillar of flesh, surprised that they could circle around it despite its diameter. I'd never felt a man's penis before. The touch beneath my fingers was hot, velvety, and pulsating. I knew exactly where I wanted it. The hollowness inside me was crying out for it. I need to be sated by him. Totally consumed.

With growing confidence, I angled it upward toward the opening between my legs. I slid the tip inside. He gave it a sharp thrust, jettisoning his member deep inside me. I let out a shriek. The initial pain and shock of the hard fullness was enough to make me almost fall off the sink or into it, but as my muscles relaxed, it felt good. Like it belonged and had found its home sweet home.

"Oh baby, you're so tight." Rolling his tongue over his lips, he gripped my hips and lifted me off the sink basin so that we were almost face to face. My feet dangled like a rag doll's, not touching the floor below.

"Wrap your legs around me," he ordered, pressing his hard body close to mine.

In no condition to argue, I did what he said, wrapping my long legs around his lean, torso like a pretzel. He gripped my thighs. My arms swung around his neck, and I squeezed him tightly, clasping the rich fabric of his suit jacket between my fingers. This was one ride I did not want to fall off.

Pressing me firmly against the bathroom wall,

he thrust his stone-hard member deeper into me, and I gasped with a mixture of shock and ecstasy as the tip rammed against a hypersensitive spot. He groaned. He slid his rod down and then thrust it upward again, this time even harder against the bull's eye. I moaned. He groaned louder. He repeated the pattern, speeding it up with every in and out. How could that giant thing between his legs fit so easily and comfortably inside me? Every thrust elicited a moan from me louder than the one before and a groan from him, deeper than the previous. I moved my arms to his buttocks, folding them firmly around the rock-hard cheeks under his trousers and fell into the rhythm of his in-and-out movements. Our breathing grew ragged.

"Oh baby, what you do to me," he groaned, his voice an octave deeper and sexy beyond belief.

"Don't stop," I pleaded, my voice breathy, my mouth dry.

"Don't worry."

He planted his thumb back on my clit and massaged it vigorously as his member glided up and down my flooded tunnel, hitting that mega-spot again and again. My temperature was rising. Sweat was pouring out of every crevice of my body. Squeezing my legs tighter around him, I closed my eyes to savor the unbearable pleasure this gorgeous beast was giving me.

"Are you on birth control?" The words drifted through my head, not expecting them. I managed a throaty "yeah" as he thrust his member once again into my tunnel of joy. I had been on the pill for several years due to my irregular cycle.

"Good, baby," he murmured in my ear. He yanked back my head by my ponytail and rolled his hot, velvety tongue up my neck. So, this was my reward for the right answer. The sensation drove me crazy. I felt like a puppy being scratched in her favorite spot.

He accelerated his pace, of both the banging and massaging. Whimpering, I didn't think I could take it anymore. My sex throbbed as a wildfire raced through my body, shamelessly kindling every nerve inside me, from my head to my toes. I was about to implode.

Without warning, I felt him exploding. "Oh, Saarah," he groaned, drawing out my name. I convulsed around him, my own deep explosion sending waves of ecstasy throughout me. *Oh my God. Oh my God. Oh my God.* I wasn't sure if I was saying the words aloud or screaming them silently in my head. What was happening to me? I had never had such a mind-blowing experience.

Slowly, he pulled out of me. I was surprised at how big and rigid his now glistening member still was. He grabbed a paper towel from the dispenser, cleaned himself up, and then adjusted his pants over his thick length. I don't think he was wearing underwear either.

"Saarah," he said as he zipped up his fly. "Do you still have to pee?"

"Yes," I stammered, as I pulled up the remains of my pantyhose and slipped on my skirt. I was shaking, dazed, and drained from his plundering.

Trainman rolled his eyes and then let me pee in peace. And privacy.

After latching the door, I got back dressed and sat on the toilet longer than I needed to. Tremors tore through me. I gazed down at a big rip in my pantyhose, in the so-called "reinforced" crotch area. A translucent, creamy substance coated my inner thighs. The events that had just happened reeled around in my head while orgasmic vibrations were still coming at me with recklessness of a rockslide. Why did I let myself do this? Why? Neediness? Insecurity? Maybe a desperate escape from the anguish my dying mother was causing? Or just because this man was the sexiest member of the opposite sex I'd ever laid my eyes on? Finally, I tore off a generous piece of toilet paper and wiped by bottom from front to back just like my mother had taught me. A translucent layer of ruby-veined semen clustered on the soft white paper. I was bleeding. Reality hit me like a brick. I had just lost my virginity to a stranger on a train.

In a state of mild shock, I slowly raised myself from the toilet, pulled up my damp, crotchless hose, and washed my hands in the sink that now held so many memories for me. I splattered a little of the cold water on my face and sipped some from my hands to quench my parched mouth. For the first time, I looked at myself in the mirror. My reflection startled me. My hair was disheveled; my big brown eyes half-moons, and my full-lipped mouth locked in a parted pout. I was no longer the girl who only minutes ago had almost been squished by a pair of automatic train doors. I looked like a woman. A woman who had just been fucked. Big time.

Hastily, I fixed my ponytail and threw some more

water on my face. I glimpsed myself again in the mirror. Not too much better, but, at least, better. Taking a deep breath, I unlatched the door and made my way back to my seat. My body was quivering. Especially the part between my inner thighs.

Trainman smiled when he saw me. I was shocked by how put together he looked, his golden hair neatly back in place and his blue eyes twinkling. Maybe he was a pro at this—snacking on some nice innocent girl on his ride home.

This time in true gentleman fashion, he rose from his seat and let me sidle to mine with a modicum of grace. We were back to sitting side by side.

As the speeding train passed through different neighborhoods, from the poorest to the toniest, we shared a self-imposed silence. Whatever we were thinking in our heads was enough to keep us entertained. I wondered... who was this man... what did he do... why did he choose me? Words stayed trapped in my throat. I swiveled my head sideways and stared at his gorgeous, high-cheekboned profile that showed off his long eyelashes, strong chin, and fine Roman nose. What was he thinking? The impassive look on his face made his thoughts unreadable, and it frustrated me..

The delicious, constant throbbing inside me would not die down, and in fact, intensified with the friction of the zooming train over the tracks. Overwhelmed with a mixture of bewilderment, awe, and a touch of guilt, my eyelids grew heavy. I set my comfy leather chair into a reclining position while Trainman pulled out his iPhone from his briefcase and caught up on emails. His skilled hands moved quickly on the touch screen keyboard. God, he was good with those fingers! Unable to read what he was writing, I peered out the window and soaked in the scenery. Before long, I could no longer keep my eyes open and drifted off.

"Last stop, New York Penn Station." The loud announcement woke me with a startle. I blinked open my eyes, to find my head resting on Trainman's broad shoulder.

"I'm sorry," I said, collecting myself.

"Don't be." He gave me a quick dimpled smile that rendered me breathless.

He helped me to my feet. "Ladies first."

As I side-stepped past him and made my way to the automatic sliding doors, the sinking feeling that I might never see him again set in.

Penn Station was stinking hot and bustling with commuters and tourists, and it wasn't even summer yet. It tasted, smelled, and sounded like 30th Street Station's ugly stepsister. Trainman clasped my hand as we wove our way in and out of the bustling crowd of rush hour commuters and ubiquitous homeless. His hand was warm, the grip firm but not too tight. I quickened my pace to keep up with him, his stride a blend of grace and arrogance. He was clearly an expert on manipulating this oppressive swarm of people. Despite having lived in the city for almost two years and taking my share of subways, I had yet to master the ruthless New Yorkers always in a hurry to get where they were going.

Half way through the station, a sharp tug from behind me followed by a forceful shove sent me crashing to the filthy Penn Station floor. Dazed, I caught my assailant, a skinny Latino youth, running through the crowd with my bag. My life! My cell phone! My wallet! My identity! And the cash I needed to get through the weekend!

"Little fucker!" yelled Trainman, taking off in hot pursuit.

Staggering to my feet, my eyes could not believe the speed with which his long legs carried him. It was like watching a scene from *Mission Impossible* with Tom Cruise or some stunt double running after the bad guy. My assailant glanced back at Trainman, panic washing over his face as he saw my action hero gaining ground. Even as the bad guy picked up speed, the gap narrowed until Trainman pounced him, sending him crashing to the floor. He lay sprawled on the floor, between Trainman's powerful straddled knees, his face frozen with fear.

I hurried toward them. Gripping the lad by a clump of his greasy ebony hair, Trainman yanked him to his feet. The boy was shaking and near tears, and I was taken by how slight he was compared to my tall, mighty, broad-shouldered hero. The boy surrendered my bag and defensively raised both hands, clearly afraid that his captor might strike him. Still clasping his hair, Trainman lifted the youth until his Nikes no longer touched the ground. The boy grimaced in pain. And then Trainman lowered him. I was close enough to hear Trainman growl, "Now, get the fuck out here." He released the boy, who, wasting no time, sprinted through the crowd without looking back.

Trainman wheeled around, his eyes searching the crowd until they landed on me. I stopped dead in my tracks. I was shaking—unsure if it was from the shock of being violated or the shock that this gorgeous man had risked his life for me—I mean, the kid could have had a knife. Taking long strides, he headed my way.

"You okay?" he asked, his blue eyes surveying every inch of my body.

"Yeah," I managed. Glancing down, I noticed that there were patches of dust on my calf-length beige skirt. My right knee hurt from the fall. I lifted up the hem of the skirt to check it out. No blood. Just a large hole in my pantyhose—though it was a mere fraction of the hole between my crotch. Embarrassment crept through me.

Ari handed me my bag, intact and in one piece. "Hold on to this," he said, his frown curling into a wry, but oh-so-sexy smile.

I quirked a quick smile back. My gaze met his once again, and I was immediately aware of the waves of ecstasy crashing against my pelvis. My heart thudded. Thank goodness the hum of the crowded station drowned out the sound in my ears.

"I'm having drinks with someone," he said.

He needed to say no more. He was meeting some gorgeous supermodel. The type of woman he belonged with. My heart sunk. It was time for my exit line.

"Um, okay," I spluttered. "Thanks for everything."
Yes, everything.

Without saying good-bye, I hastily headed toward

an Exit sign. I walked blindly through the throng of rush-hour commuters and homeless, brushing up against more than I wanted. It was over. My scenes from a movie were over. I didn't even know a thing about him. His last name. Where he lived. What he did. What did it matter? I'd probably never see him again. It was just a fluke thing that wasn't supposed to happen to me. I shrugged my shoulders and inwardly sighed. Yet, there was so much of me that kept hoping I would feel his strong hands on my shoulders, stopping me dead in my tracks. Spinning me around. Pulling my head back with a yank of my ponytail. Sinking his lips into mine and then parting them with his tongue, inviting me for a smoochy dance right in the middle of Penn Station. That's what happened in movies. With wishful thinking, I stole a glance backward. Trainman was hugging a tall, shapely, drop-dead gorgeous redhead in a chic suit. Just his type. I hastily pivoted around and quickened my pace. Why was I fooling myself? My *West Side Story* was a dream. My life was a reality show. A really lame reality show.

2

I DECIDED TO WALK HOME FROM Penn Station. The furnished apartment I was subletting on West Forty-Fifth Street between Eighth and Ninth Avenues on the edge of the theater district was not far. Besides, it was a warm May night, and I needed the air to clear my head. Unfortunately, the intense throbbing in my groin area kept me in a fog. Trainman's beautiful face filled my mind while his beautiful dick filled every other part of me. And then the image of that stunning redhead made it all go away faster than losing my virginity. The reality that I was no longer "the twenty-five-year-old virgin" as Lauren sarcastically called me made me shudder with disbelief. It had to happen sometime, but now I had twinges of regret that it had happened with that Adonis. A stranger on a train.

Mounting the five-step landing that led to my brownstone apartment, I dug deep into my messenger bag in search of my keys and sighed with relief when I found them. Had it not been for Trainman, I would have had no bag or keys. For all I know, that kid, having access to my identity and address, might have vandalized my apartment and wiped out everything. And if I happened to be home at the time, who knows what else might have happened. I trembled, thinking about the possibilities.

I jiggled the keys into the double metal locks, struggling with one after another. It was a royal pain in the butt to open the front door, but one could never be too safe in this big city, especially in my neighborhood which was still considered a little seedy.

Once inside, I used a tiny key attached to the chain to open one of three tarnished metal mailboxes that lined the chipped entryway. Two other tenants lived in the building—Mrs. Blumberg, on the second floor, a retired Broadway actress who always had a story about her song and dance days to tell me and was convinced she was related to the mayor, and Mr. Costanzo, on the ground floor, who owned a pizzeria and was always trying to feed me. My apartment, identical to theirs, was located on the third floor.

Bills. Bills. And more bills. Including one from The Hospital of the University of Pennsylvania. I would deal with all of them later. Right now, I had to hurry and get myself ready for the Black Eyed Peas concert in Central Park. Perhaps some good music and food would get my mind off my sick mother and the sick feeling I had about never seeing Trainman again.

Usually the trek up the steep three flights of stairs was effortless for me, but this evening it was challenging. I was worn out, my insides torn both physically and emotionally. As I mounted each step, the image of my mother, wan and frail, life ebbing out of her alternated with the image of Ari, tan and fit, putting life into me. I could still feel his hot pulsing member deep inside me. I wanted it go away and move on. *Liar.* I wanted more of him.

Breathing heavily, I unlocked the double locks of my apartment door after several attempts. Jo-Jo, the sweet black cat I was caring for while his (her?—I wasn't sure) true owner, a flamboyant singing-dancing transvestite, partook in year-long tour of *La Cage Aux Folles,* immediately brushed up against my ankles and meowed.

The flat, a railroad apartment, was small but pleasant. I was lucky to have found it on Craigslist. It was rent-controlled, so I wasn't paying much, and the tenant even gave me a small break for looking after Jo-Jo. The only thing odd about the apartment was that the walls were painted hot pink, and there was a large framed photo of Josephine Baker (the inspiration for kitty's name?) above the pseudo-Victorian sofa. The other flea market finds that filled the apartment gave it a quirky charm that appealed to me.

Jo-Jo followed me into the small galley kitchen, where I proceeded to open a can of Fancy Feast and put it into his special bowl on the Formica counter. I'd better check my phone messages; it had been a while.

I pushed play on the answering machine that sat on the other end of the counter. Lauren: "Where are you?" CLICK. Lauren: "What are you wearing? Remember, my cotillion friends are coming." CLICK. Lauren: "Where are you?" CLICK. Lauren: "Guess what! Taylor is taking me to The Hamptons." CLICK. Lauren: "Call me!" CLICK. Lauren: "FYI, your cell phone is turned off."

No more messages. My heart sunk. So much of me wanted to hear Trainman's sultry voice. "Saarah. Call me. I want to make you wet and fuck your brains out."

Stop it, Sarah! I silently chided. He was probably already bedding that beautiful redhead. And he had no idea where I lived or how to get in touch with me. Chances were I'd never see or hear from him again. Yet, the raw aching I felt for this man continued to consume me.

Enough. I'd better call Lauren and let her know that I was back in town and that I would meet her at her at the Seventy-Second Street entrance to the park at 7:30. As I reached for my phone, the buzzer on my intercom sounded. Lately, any time it did, my heart dropped to the floor, thinking it might be someone serving me for non-payment of bills. Or even worse, some messenger with the news of my mother's passing. Nervously, I pressed the button and talked into the intercom. "Yes?" My voice trailed off.

"Delivery for you," said a male voice with a heavy New York accent.

That was strange. I wasn't expecting anything. Unless my new evil boss had decided to send a stack of her expenses to take care of over the weekend. I had taken the day off to visit my mother, and she was not one bit happy about it. So, this was her revenge.

I pushed the button on the intercom that unlocked the front door. "Just leave it on the stairs."

"You need to sign for it," said the invisible voice.

"Fine. I'll be right down."

Grabbing one of the loose pens that I kept in a tin can on the counter, I galloped down the three flights of stairs. The aftershocks of my orgasm measured 6.0 on the "I can come" scale.

Waiting for me at the base of the staircase was a twitchy man holding a box that must have measured five feet in length. It was magnificently wrapped in violet paper and topped off with a white bow the size of a basketball. This could not possibly be for me.

"Sign this," said the man, handing me a receipt. Sure enough my name, Sarah Greene, was printed on the paper along with my address and apartment number. Huh? And then it hit me. Of course, it was a gift from my mega-wealthy debutante friend Lauren, who probably sent me something nice to wear to the concert tonight so I wouldn't be an embarrassment in front of all her high society friends. She had threatened to burn my entire wardrobe once, and this was her way of sending me a message.

Grabbing the receipt, I plastered it against the hallway wall and signed my name. The deliveryman promptly left, and I humped the stairs with the large package in my arms. What did Lauren pick out for me? Knowing her over-the-top expensive taste, I'm sure it was something like Seven for Mankind tight-ass jeans and some Roberto Cavalli bold print halter-top cut so low you could see my navel. Trendy things that flat-chested, straight-as-an-arrow, bohemian me had no right wearing. And would not look good in.

Once back inside my apartment, I gently laid the massive package on the couch and carefully unwrapped it. I'd never seen such a meticulously wrapped present, and the dazzling bow must have cost a small fortune. Lauren could afford it. Her father, Randolph Hoffmeier, was a major Wall Street CEO, and she already had a substantial trust fund from her Mayflower-descended family.

The box was from Bergdorf's. Wow! The only time I'd ever set foot inside that store was the one time my new bitch boss sent me there at lunch to pick up a tube of her favorite Chanel red lipstick. Dressed in my cheap version of bohemian whatever, I stuck out like a sore thumb among all the expensively dressed and scented women and couldn't wait to get out of the place. I spent the rest of my lunch break down the street consoling myself at T.J. Maxx.

I carefully removed the box top. Layers of delicate tissue paper lined the interior of the other half. I peeled them away, and then I gasped. Facing me was a beautifully folded black silk dress with two sparkling spaghetti straps. A tag hung off one of them. Marc Jacobs. Size 6. No price. I lifted the dress by the straps and held it up in front of me. It was gorgeous. Simple but elegant. But certainly not the kind of thing one would wear to a rock concert in Central Park. What was Lauren thinking?

My eyes returned to the box and came upon a small white envelope with my name printed on it. Draping the dress over an arm, I reached for it and pulled out the contents from under the unsealed flap. My eyes grew big as I read the note and so did the explosions that were rocking my body.

Ms. Greene~

*Please wear this tonight. I'll collect you at 8
p.m. Please be downstairs.*

~Ari

PS Please do not wear pantyhose.

A mixture of holy cow and damn him saturated
my brain. How the heck did he know where I lived?
Wait. Of course, the stalker must have gone through
my messenger bag while I was dozing on that damn
train. He got my address from my driver's license.
He must know everything about me. My height.
My weight. My checking account number with my
home phone number. My social security number.
What kind of gum I chewed (Big Red). Crap. I bet he
even thumbed through my sketchpad and read the
journal I kept with my favorite sayings.

One of them flashed into my head. *"When in
doubt, leave it out."* Damn it! I should have never
let him sink his cock inside me. None of this would
have happened. None of it. Except... there was no
doubt. I had wanted him as much as he had wanted
me.

And now there was another problem. I couldn't
see him tonight. I had plans with Lauren. Trust me,
she rubbed it my face that she was able to get those
reserved-seating Black Eyed Peas tickets because
her father's investment company managed Fergie's
assets and that I was lucky that she counted me as
one of her best friends.

The shrill ring of my phone hurled me out of my thoughts. It must be Lauren. I dreaded answering it because she got super mad if I didn't call her back right away. For a friend, she was very high maintenance.

Finally, after the fifth ring, just before the call went to my answering machine, I ran over to it and picked up the receiver.

"Saarah, do you like your dress?"

Yikes! It was him. The temperature in the kitchen suddenly rose ten degrees.

"It's very nice." Who was I kidding? It was the most fabulous dress I'd ever owned. And the most expensive.

"I'm looking forward to seeing you in it."

Shit! How the hell was I going to tell him that I had plans? That I couldn't see him tonight.

CLICK.

I wasn't. I immediately dialed Lauren's number. Her answering machine was on. *Beep.*

"Lauren, something's come up. I can't go to the concert tonight. I'll explain tomorrow. Have fun."

CLICK. Phew! That saved me from having a nasty, drawn-out conversation with her. I suppose I could also try her on her cell, but truthfully, I didn't want to. And I wasn't feeling that guilty. She had her entourage. I'd still pay the consequences tomorrow, but right now, I had to get ready for my date with Trainman.

Taking my new dress with me, I loped toward the bedroom that was adjacent to the living room. A loud knock at my door stopped me in the hallway. Retracing my steps, I peered through the peephole.

Mrs. Blumberg. She was rather entertaining, but quite frankly, I had no time for her right now.

I unbolted the door.

Chewing a big wad of gum, she said in her thick "New Yawk" accent, "I was just on my way to shul when this came for you." She handed me a shopping bag. Inside was another gift-wrapped package, this one significantly smaller, maybe a foot long by six inches. My heart fluttered. Now what?

Mrs. Blumberg's crinkly eyes fixated on the black dress that was still folded over my arm. "You have yourself a date tonight? I hope he's Jewish."

God, she was nosy. And so annoying. I didn't respond.

"So, how's your mother doing?"

Sadness swept over me. After I left the hospital, my mother was scheduled for another treatment. They always made her feel sicker than she already was. I fought back tears.

"She's hanging in there."

"*Oy!*" She shook her head, a bright-orange ball of frizz. "I'll say a prayer for her tonight."

"Thanks." Mrs. Blumberg meant well. It was hard not to like her even though she could be annoying.

"So, what are you waiting for? You gonna show me whatch'ya got?"

God, she was being difficult.

"Mrs. Blumberg, I'd love to spend time with you but—"

"I know. I know. It's okay to hurt an old lady's feelings. You gotta hot date."

Her voice trailed off as she shuffled to the door to my apartment. Closing it behind her, she got in her last two cents. "Make sure you wear clean underwear. And don't let him touch you there."

Too late! "There" tingled with the thought of being touched by "him" again. Wasting no time, I reached into the shopping bag and tore the package open. Two words on the lid of the shiny white box blazed in my eyes: JIMMY CHOO. I lifted the lid to find another note, the sexy, bold handwriting identical to that of the note that accompanied the black dress.

> *Wear these tonight. Remember, no pantyhose.~A*

Holy cow! He bought me shoes? The kind you see in *Vogue* and the copy says: "Price on Request." A creamy white duster bag encased the shoes. My heart thudding, I removed the shoes. I gasped. A pair of six-inch high black satin peep-toe pumps. Size 9.5AA. How the hell did he know my crazy shoe size? Did he remove my two-sizes-too-wide combat boots stuffed with inner sole pads to make them fit while I was dozing on the train?

A horrifying thought crossed my mind. I was born wearing combat boots. How was I going to manage to walk in these sexy beasts? I took off my boots and placed the high heels side by side on the floor. Placing one hand flat against the wall, I stepped into them, right foot, then left. Sarah, plain and tall, was suddenly taller. Six inches taller. A 6'2" pillar.

I let go of the wall. Okay, I could balance in them. But could I walk in them? I was going to do my trial runway walk down the hallway to my bedroom. Still carrying the little black dress, I took my first step, then my next. My ankles wobbled, and the intense throbbing inside me was not doing anything to help my balance. *Focus, Sarah. Focus.* Pausing for a deep breath, I took another step and then another... I was getting it down. My bedroom was just an arm's length away. Victoriously, I stumbled inside it. Jo-Jo, whom I'd honestly forgotten about, followed right behind me.

My shoebox-size bedroom, painted in another shade of hot pink, consisted of a queen-size bed that took up most of the space, faux-French mirrored armoire, matching nightstand and a sliver of a closet. Jo-Jo jumped up on the bed and curled up on the garish leopard-print satin sheets left behind by the transvestite. Not wanting the dress near the furry cat, I draped it over my closet door. I glanced at the alarm clock on my nightstand. 7:15 p.m. I had less than an hour to get ready for my date. Quickly, I slipped out of my peasant skirt, letting it fall to the floor. As I pulled my t-shirt over my head, a waft of his cologne drifted into my nose. God, he smelled so divine. Maybe, I should never wash this t-shirt. Hold on to it as keepsake. A souvenir of losing my virginity.

Wearing my torn pantyhose and my six-inch Jimmy's, I stood before the armoire and gazed at my reflection in the mirror. My normally long legs seemed to go on for miles. The heels accentuated my calf muscles and toned thighs, both gifts of having been a tomboy my whole life. I ran my palms over my pert champagne-cup breasts, surprised by the soreness of my small nipples. The memory of Trainman nipping and tugging them filled my head. An electric current surged through my body.

Holding onto the armoire, I removed my new shoes and slid down my pantyhose. I had the urge to hold them to my nose, but I let them scrunch on the floor. Maybe, I should put them in a zip lock baggie and hide them in the armoire. The scene from an episode of *Law and Order* popped into my head, as if losing your virginity to a stranger on a train was a crime. Jack McCoy: "Your honor, I present to the court Exhibit A: Defendant's Cum-Soaked Pantyhose."

Inwardly chuckling, I headed, naked, to the hole-in-the-wall bathroom located off the small hallway that connected the living room and bedroom. I turned on the water and hopped into the narrow, tiled stall shower and, with misgivings, let the warm water wash away the residue of my Trainman encounter. I lathered my hair with shampoo and rubbed my soapy hand between my legs, shocked that the bud hidden in the folds was so sensitive and engorged.

After conditioning my mid-back length hair, I stepped out of the shower and wrapped a towel around me—a leopard print one that matched the satin sheets on the bed. I glanced at my reflection in the medicine cabinet mirror. My too-big-for-my-face chocolate eyes were a little bloodshot from my lack of sleep, but my skin was glowing, and I thanked my lucky stars for the zillionth time that I had been blessed with good skin. The genes of my mother. My heart grew heavy again—the image of her once radiant face, now sunken and sallow, filled my mind. I wondered how her treatment went. I so badly wanted to call her, but usually after one of them, she was weak and nauseated and preferred to talk to no one. Not even me, her only daughter. Her best friend and confidant. How I missed my mother!

With a weighty sigh, I threw my soaked chestnut hair into a ponytail and dabbed on some berry-flavored lip-gloss, something I rarely did. The thought of Trainman licking it off my lips made me tingle. I hadn't been kissed by him. Fucked. But not kissed. What would that be like? At last minute, I spritzed myself with perfume. Sarah Jessica Parker's Lovely, a birthday present from Lauren.

I headed back to my bedroom and beheld the little black dress, waiting for my body to claim it. Careful not to get my lip-gloss on it, I slipped it over my head, squeezed my arms under the spaghetti straps and pulled it down. It stopped mid-thigh and fit my body like a glove, giving me little curves I never thought I had. The silky fabric was cool and soothing against my skin. I pulled off the tag and tossed it into the waste can. Jo-Jo gave me the cat's meow. Marc Jacobs and I were now one.

"Don't wear pantyhose." I could hear his sexy voice saying the words. Okay, so panties it would be. I opened the door to my armoire and pulled out a pair from the narrow drawer where I kept my collection of Fruit of the Looms. Cheap, comfy white panties I bought on sale at the downtown Target. I slipped my feet into the leg openings and slid them up under my dress. I stared at myself in the mirror. Damn! I had panty lines. Ugly panty lines.

"Remember, no pantyhose." Fine. I'd live with the

lines, but silently I cursed my Fruit of the Looms, wishing that I had a single pair of those obnoxious butt-floss thongs. I slipped my bare feet back into my black satin Jimmy's and gave a final look at myself in the mirror.

Sarah, plain and tall in her little black dress and grown-up high heels, no longer looked plain but instead borderline elegant. More *West Side Story* lyrics floated in my head. *"See the pretty girl in the mirror there."* But, damn, damn, damn, those panty lines. They were ruining everything. Impulsively, I reached my under my dress and yanked the panties down, letting them slide down to my ankles. I kicked them off, almost losing my balance.

The phone in the kitchen rang. My answering machine picked up. I could faintly hear Lauren's voice; The Black Eyed Peas were singing "I've Gotta Feeling" in the background. "Sarah, what the fuck is going on? Call me immediately." CLICK.

I glanced again at my alarm clock. 7:55 p.m. Lauren would have to wait. Pantyless, I, Sarah Greene, was ready for my next encounter with my mysterious Trainman.

8:00 p.m. I stood anxiously on the landing of my apartment. My eyes darted east and west, searching for a tall, golden-haired Adonis that stood out from the crowd. A melting pot of New Yorkers passed me by, several pausing to stare. A silver-haired businessman gave me a wink, and a rapper type gave me a thumbs-up wolf whistle. I wasn't used to being noticed, let alone winked and whistled at. It was as empowering as it was embarrassing.

My nerves grew edgier by the minute. What if he was going to stand me up? The image of the beautiful redhead flickered once more in my head. I always said, *"The grass can't compete with the trees."* I was just a blade of grass in a big city filled with beautiful women.

My heart was sinking, and my inner vibrations were ticking like a countdown clock. And then as I was about to lose all hope, my eyes caught sight of my long-legged Trainman running down the street in my direction. He loped up the landing, taking two steps at a time. A cocky grin flashed across his face.

My heart did a happy dance at the sight of him. He was dressed in jeans—the expensive, premium denim kind—and a black cotton tee—the expensive, yummy kind. I immediately felt overdressed in his LBD and uncomfortable.

"Hi," I said nervously. I hated myself for my banality.

In my six-inch heels, we were practically the same height. His piercing blue eyes burned into mine and then traveled down my body, lingering on places he had no right to be. "The dress suits you," he said at last with a glimmer of approval.

He offered me his arm, and my eyes fixed on his biceps. Perfect, not too big to shout professional weight lifter but enough to let me know that he worked out. The rest of his body was equally sculpted to perfection. The outlines of his muscled thighs and calves were visible through the denim, and I could see the ripple of his abs beneath his fine cotton tee.

I hooked my arm in his, glad to have someone help me down the steps in these mile-high heels. *Please don't let me trip. Please!* I prayed silently.

I made it to the street. A small victory. I suppose we were walking somewhere—there were lots of good restaurants in the theater district—but truthfully, I was not looking forward to walking more than a block in my Jimmy's. My feet were already beginning to ache, and I still did not trust myself in them.

"My driver will be here any second," said Trainman.

Driver? What was he talking about? In a heartbeat, a sleek black limo slithered up to us. Trainman motioned with his finger to it and helped me step off the curb.

A tall uniformed man with rich ebony skin and the intimidating build of Mr. Clean immediately came around the car and opened the backdoor.

"After you," said Trainman.

I looked at him with hesitancy, and then with as much grace as I could muster in my tight black dress and six-inch high Jimmy's, I slid into the car. Trainman climbed in after me. The passenger door closed, and I was sitting once again next to my mysterious stranger on a train.

The posh, spacious interior felt alien to me. Rich black leather seats, plush carpeting, dark-tinted windows, plus a dark glass partition separating the two of us from the driver. There was also a well-stocked bar. I'd never been in a limo before. Obviously, Trainman was rich. *Very* rich. Again the question: What was he doing with me?

He stretched his long, taut legs out in front of him, and I noticed he was wearing expensive black loafers, with no socks. I impulsively crossed mine—acutely aware that I wasn't wearing underwear. The thought made me press by legs tighter together. I wondered—was this some kind of defense mechanism?

Trainman glanced down at my crotch—holy shit, did he know?—and then subtly down at my feet. A sly smile flickered on his tanned face. Was it the beautiful shoes or the fact that I was not wearing pantyhose that pleased him? I dared not to ask.

The scent of his expensive cologne, mixed with that of the car's rich leather, wafted up my nose, making me feel light-headed. Butterflies fluttered in my stomach, and the throbbing in my core kicked up a notch with the movement of the car. *Please don't let me get carsick.*

"I hope you like lobster," he said, breaking the silence.

Oooh. That was a conversation starter. Me, who lived on ramen noodles and an occasional macrobiotic dinner out, courtesy of BFF Lauren, who was forever going through a raw diet phase, didn't know the first thing about eating lobster. All I knew was that it was a big red shellfish with big, scary claws that I could never afford.

"Yes," I lied.

"Good. We're going to The Palm, my favorite restaurant."

"Cool."

This was not going well. Despite my intimate encounter with this gorgeous man only a few hours ago, I now felt at a loss for words. Remembering one of my favorite sayings, *"Speak only when spoken to,"* I peered out the tinted window, gazing at the spectacle of cars, cabs, and pedestrians that made New York the city that never sleeps. A thought crossed my mind. I could see them, but they could not see me. Somehow, I thought Trainman's piercing blue eyes could see right through me yet mine could not penetrate him. He made me feel naked.

Trainman's voice diverted my attention. "Would you like a drink?"

"Um, a coke would be nice."

Trainman smirked. He reached for a bottle of wine, already uncorked, and poured some into two crystal goblets. He handed me a glass and then clinked his against mine.

"Cheers. To you and a fine meal." His eyes stayed fixed on my face.

I put the goblet to my lips and took a sip of the wine. It was chilled and delicious. It didn't taste like the acidic or oversweet "house wine" I occasionally ordered when I was out with Lauren. No, it tasted perfectly balanced and velvety. I glanced at the label on the bottle; it was in French. So, Trainman liked fine cars, fine wines, fine food... and fine women?

The limo was heading east across Forty-Second Street, the driver expertly weaving in and out of the insane Friday night midtown traffic. I imbibed more of my wine.

"So, Saarah..."

There he was saying my name with that slow sexy lilt. My breath caught in my throat.

Holding the glass of wine in one hand, he slowly

ran the manicured fingertips of the other down my right leg, all the way down to my ankle. His caress gave me goose bumps.

"...You didn't wear any pantyhose," he purred, his hand rubbing up and down my ankle.

I swallowed hard. I was too nervous to say anything.

"I hope you're as hungry as I am."

"I'm famished," I squeaked. Suddenly, I was craving a heaping portion of his cock. My stomach emitted an embarrassing growl.

He responded with that bemused smile.

His hand glided back up my leg and made its way under the silky satin of my little black dress. His middle finger toyed with my button. I was getting hot. Very hot. And very wet.

"You're salivating. You *must* be starving."

I bit down on my berry-stained lips to suppress a moan.

"Open your mouth," he growled.

Hesitantly, I parted my lips. Removing his hand from between thighs, he slid his middle finger, wet with my sex, across my tongue. "Just a small taste of what's to come."

I steadied the wine in my hand. I feared one way or another I was going to end up with a large wet stain on my stunning black dress if we didn't get to the restaurant soon.

The limo turned north on Third Avenue and, after a couple of turns, pulled up behind a cab in front of The Palm. The driver got out and the door opened. Trainman slid out and I followed, aided by his hand. I really was hungry.

Inside, The Palm was a noisy, bustling restaurant with white-clothed tables and a colorful array of caricatures of well-known celebrities lining the walls. At the reception area, a jovial heavyset man, with half-moon glasses, who looked to be in his late sixties, greeted Trainman with a warm handshake.

"Good to see you, Mr. Golden. Your regular table is waiting for you."

So now, I knew Trainman's full name. Ari Golden. Fitting for the golden-haired warrior. Later tonight, I would google him and find out everything there was to know.

Holding my hand, Ari followed an attractive, mini-skirted hostess who kept looking back at him, past the jammed bar and table after table of chicly dressed couples and businessmen devouring lobsters. I managed to keep up on my heels and again prayed I wouldn't do something embarrassing like breaking my ankle in front of all these diners.

Several stunning, well-dressed women stopped Ari along the way, eyeing me curiously. Ari politely acknowledged each of them with a quick smile and a nod. *Former strangers on a train?*

The booth to which we were led was in the far corner of the restaurant. It could easily accommodate four more people, but we had it all to ourselves. I sat on one side, Ari on the other.

A waiter came by shortly, and Ari ordered for the two of us. Two Manhattans, Caesar salad, and a four-pound lobster to share.

I was happy when the Manhattans arrived at our table. I still felt super-nervous in front of this man. I didn't know what to talk about. I took several consecutive gulps of the drink—another first. The velvety cold liquid went down smoothly and loosened me up. A little.

Twirling his Manhattan cherry by the stem, Ari eased into conversation. "Sarah is a beautiful name. It means 'princess' in Hebrew."

My mother had told me that once, but I was the last thing from being a princess. Tomboy, geek, plain Jane, yes. But not princess. "Thanks," I said in a tone that was more dubious than flattered.

He plucked the cherry from his drink and flicked it with his tongue. "I've seen you many times before at 30th Street Station."

I gulped. He had been spying on me? He really was a stalker.

"Were you visiting someone there?" He popped the cherry into his mouth and swallowed.

I nervously nodded.

"Oh, a boyfriend?"

"No, my mom," I replied, taken aback by his question. "She's being treated for cancer at The Hospital of the University of Pennsylvania."

All the emotions I had bottled up broke loose. I don't know what caused it. The wine. The Manhattan. The cherry. Or a combination of all three. Tears that had been welling up in my eyes on and off all day streamed down my cheeks.

Before I could apologize for my emotional outbreak, Ari leaned into me and brushed them away with his thumbs. With a tenderness that surprised me.

"I'm sorry," I sniffed.

"Don't be." His voice embodied genuine

compassion. "I lost my father to cancer several years ago."

So we had something in common. Or close enough. Fingers crossed, my mother would go into remission.

"What kind?" I asked hesitantly.

"Lung." Sadness filled his voice. "He was a smoker."

"My mother has lung cancer too, but she never smoked a day in her life." Anger from this unfair fate rose fast and furious inside me. Just in time, the Caesar salads arrived. I picked at mine, my appetite suddenly gone. Trainman dug into his, sheepishly gazing up at me with each forkful.

"Saarah, cheer up!" It was almost a command. "Here comes the lobster."

My eyes grew wide at the sight of the monstrous red-shelled creature that our waiter set down in the center of our table. On either side of the platter, he placed a couple of nutcrackers and pickers. Tying ample plastic bibs around our necks, he bid us, *"Bon appétit."*

My anxious eyes darted back and forth between the lobster and Ari's face. I had never eaten a lobster before and had no clue where to begin.

He was a god. And a mind reader. "Watch. Use the nutcracker and start with the tail. The most succulent part." Squeezing the utensil, he skillfully cracked the creature's tail and then plunged one of the slim two-pronged forks into the meat. "Taste," he ordered after dipping the snowy meat into a side of melted butter.

I opened my mouth and let him feed me the

buttery piece of lobster meat. Oh, God, it was good. Rich, melt-in-your-mouth good. I instantly wanted more.

"Your turn." A wry smile curled on his face. "But, I want you to crack a claw. The next best piece of meat."

Taking the nutcracker, I wrapped it around one of the lobster's large claws. I pressed hard, but the shell would not crack

Suddenly, under the table, I felt Ari grab at a naked calf. He pulled off my Jimmy Choo and moved my foot to the crotch of his expensive jeans. The sole of my foot sat directly on the warm bulge between his muscular thighs. Gripping my ankle, he rubbed my foot up and down. Slowly. Then faster. The mound hardened and expanded while my foot caught fire.

I fumbled with the nutcracker. I still couldn't crack open the damn claw. I was totally distracted.

"I'm hungry," growled Ari. He rubbed my bare foot faster and harder against his member. The rigid rod beneath his jeans tensed further. Absent-mindedly still working on the claw, I gazed at the man sitting across from me; his eyes were closed, his lush lips parted, and his back slightly arched. His member thrust deep into the arch of my foot and gave way to a spasm beneath my sole that made my toes curl.

And at that very moment, the claw cracked opened, the tender white meat inside exploding through the shell. I plunked the two-pronged fork into a chunk and slid it into Ari's parted lips. His eyes remained shut as he moaned, "Mmmm."

I delighted in the pleasure I could give this

gorgeous man.

He savored the meat in his mouth and then opened his eyes. I watched him swallow.

"My princess, that was delicious."

I flushed at his compliment. And he called me his princess!

"And now for dessert." With a hungry smile, he picked up a spoon and then accidentally on purpose dropped it. It landed under the table. "Whoops. Excuse me."

Puzzled by his behavior, I watched as he gracefully slid his sculpted body under the table to retrieve it.

Remembering my bare foot, I quickly wiggled my toes back into my shoe. A hand gripped my ankle and yanked my foot out before I could set my heel down. A moist, warm mouth descended on my big toe and sucked it up and down feverishly. Tingles shot up my leg, all the way up to my crotch. Oh my God! Dessert had arrived.

Having enough of my big toe, he nibbled and sucked the rest of them. Delicious pain followed by delicious pleasure. He bent my foot backward and moved his mouth to my heel. His tongue glided, like a slow rollercoaster across my high arch, making its way back to my toes. The sensation sent a shiver up my spine. Who knew that the soles of my feet were so sensitive?

Holding my foot in his palms, his tongue continued its journey up my long, naked leg. The sensation was ticklish, yet strangely erotic. I did some back arching of my own. When it reached my inner thigh, his hands firmly pulled my legs apart. Oh, God. Here came the icing on the cake.

Instead of the warm tongue I was expecting, the back of the spoon pressed against the folds of my pantyless crotch. The unexpected chill of the metal jolted me. He circled the spoon around my cleft, arousing me further. I clenched my fists and moaned inwardly. Oh, God. What this man could do me!

Pulling up my dress a high as it would go, he let his tongue take over. It figure skated across the surface of my folds, performing all kinds of tricks, from spins to figure eights. My patch of ice was melting, turning into one steaming hot wet river. His ever-so fit tongue stroked furiously. The pressure between my legs mounted—I wanted to scream! I bit down on my lips—*Oh, please let me come!*—and finally an explosion gave me the relief I'd been craving.

Shudders spread through me. My heart was beating madly. And then I jolted again. He pressed the cold spoon back onto my hot pulsing sex, gliding it up and down along the folds. The shock of the cold sensation intensified the fire between my legs. *Oh! Oh! Oh!*

He re-emerged from under the table, with the spoon dangling from his luscious mouth. Slowly, he removed it, sucking on it as if he were savoring the last bit of sweet creamy frosting. He languidly rolled his tongue over his moist upper lip and murmured, "Saarah, I hope you enjoyed dessert as much as I did."

"It was amazing," I gasped, still vibrating below.

His lips curved into a dimpled, satisfied smile.

I stared at his beautiful face, realizing that I still

knew so little about this man who had robbed me of my virginity and made me explode with ecstasy now more than once.

"What do you do?" I asked, finding the courage to interrogate him.

"I'm a businessman."

"So, you were on a business trip to Philadelphia today?"

"No, my company is based there. I commute back and forth every day."

That was a big distance to travel twice a day, but obviously his employer made the trip worthwhile.

"And what do you do?" he asked, his voice flirtatious.

"I work for—"

Before I could finish my sentence, Trainman leaped up from his seat.

My eyes followed him as his long legs strode to the front of the restaurant. And then my heart leapt into my throat.

The gorgeous redhead! And she was in Trainman's arms.

My emotions skipped over jealousy and sprinted straight to rage. How could he do this to me? And so shamelessly right in front of me?

Without putting on my other Jimmy, I jumped up from the table and hobbled over to them. If people were staring at me, I was oblivious. The redhead regarded me suspiciously. As if I were in a league below her and didn't belong here.

His face, however, brightened. "Saarah—"

"Don't 'Saarah' me." In a single smooth move, I yanked off my other Jimmy and flung it at him. "You can keep your damn shoes," I shouted. I stormed out the front door, pretty sure I would not be returning to The Palm any time soon. Make that ever.

With tears pouring down my face, I headed west on Forty-Fifth Street. I hadn't brought along my messenger bag with my wallet, so I was going to have to walk home barefoot. Fortunately, the night was still warm.

Tears kept coming. Past Third. Past Lexington. Past Park. Happy, laughing young couples, taking advantage of the fine weather, passed me by, but they were just a blur.

I wanted to get him out of my mind. Erase him forever. But I couldn't. The intense throbbing just would not go away. I hated him. I hated her. And hated myself most of all. How could I be so stupid to fall for this callous man? To give him my body, pure and unadulterated? To trust him? My mother had always told me to wait for someone who really loved you. She made the mistake of not—and had to raise me as a single parent. I should have listened to her words of wisdom. And right now, there was nothing I wanted more than to talk to my mother. To tell her everything. To hear her consoling words. And feel her loving embrace.

When I got home, I was going to take a scissors to his little black dress and shred it to pieces. I was going to go back to who I really was. Sarah plain and tall.

Printed in Great Britain
by Amazon